# A NOVEL

# RAGE, REFUGE, & REBELLION

## EZEKIEL ELIZALDE

Elizalde Publishing

Published by Elizalde Publishing
Kyle, TX



Distributed by EZ Publishing

Design and composition by Neil Gonzalez
Cover design by Neil Gonzalez
Cover images used under license from
©Shutterstock.com/Ninell; ©Shutterstock.com/ATTABOON
ATTHAYUWAT; ©Shutterstock.com/Black Digital Cat;
©Shutterstock.com/callumrc

Print ISBN: 979-8-9856031-0-1

First Edition

I t's the Cold War, although I'm not very cold since I am working in a pipeline that consists of gas, water, and even electrical wiring. Someone tells me that I must help them tear it down, and I agree to it because I feel obligated to do it. Once I've attempted it, I get caught. I, of all people, and another person get blamed for the operation. The man who told me to do it comes after me. I defend myself with every-thing I have, heart racing and could feel the blood rushing through my body. I don't know what to do. I later get taken away. After this whole incident, I go back to work but realize that there is a bounty on my head. My heart drops and my eyes dart around the room. My friends who I work with help me escape by giving me a note with *Weiland Harrison 4444 5555* scrawled on it. Now I start running for my life, my legs becoming weightless and my breathing heavy. I run through a food market and into a clothing shop containing jeans, jackets and shirts hung up in rows that has the name and numbers from the note. The beautiful girl I like comes and follows me inside, dark hair and blue eyes flabbergasted me. I am so relieved now that I see a friend, and we both escape out of the shop and through the market. Coming out of the market we walk through a fresh, green forest. The girl and I smile and laugh at our company peacefully. Until the people who want my bounty are here, and we're stuck in a for-est, and a deep and water-flowing ravine sits in front of us with a large wooden bridge lying across it making an arch. Once again, my heart is racing, and my thoughts are going as fast as possible. I run with the girl towards the ravine and when we get there, we jump. The air leaves my chest. Then the dream ends.

This story is based on that dream.

# DAVID

The air is warm and humid, the sound of constant banging of metal on metal rings throughout the room. Inside this large basement, there are pipes leading from left to right along the low-hanging ceiling. To the left are furnaces burning the metal into a red color. They're fueled by the large amounts of coal and gas coming from the pipes, and smoke shoots from the top. There are around six or seven of these furnaces, and each one has lines of tables with metal shrapnel lined up next to it. People are metalworking the shrapnel into blades.

But I work on the left side with all the pipes and electrical wiring. The larger pipes running along the ceiling and into the wall are the gas and water pipes used to fuel the furnaces and the appliances in the upper floors. My father and I worked here ever since I was little, probably when I was around eight years old, although I never really did much at the time. Our job was to make sure that the gas and water lines didn't have leaks, and when they did, we patched them up pretty quick. We also provided the workers with propane tanks for metal working and made sure everything was working with the wires.

All of this work was and is for the Academy. An organization that educates and trains bounty hunters who track down thieves, murderers, drug dealers, and other people. The Academy's councilmen and councilwomen believe that these people are destroying society.

I was never interested in the hunting business. That was my mother's job. My father and I just stayed in the facility, making sure everything was working properly. We observed what was going on, but we just did our jobs as we were told. I wish my father was still here working with me.

I've been doing this for about four years on my own since my parents died. I can't tell what happened since I wasn't there to witness it. All I know is that I was preparing a meal for myself at home when I heard a knock at the door. When I answered it, the head of the pipeline, Councilman Witemore, and Councilman Robins stood in the doorway with sorrowful faces. Robins was a big, stringy-haired man while Witemore was a little shorter, with white hair and beard.

Councilman Witemore said to me, "I'm sorry that I have to bring you horrible news. There is no easy way to say this, David, but your parents have passed away in an accident at the ski resort."

My heart stopped and my legs fell from beneath me. My parents had gone to the ski resort for their anniversary. That's where their first date was. To find out that they passed on the day of their marriage was heartbreaking. But I never knew the details, only that it was an accident. I begged them to tell me how it happened, and they merely said they went down the wrong path.

I was fifteen then, now I work only with my friends, Connor, Mike, and Roger. I consider Connor to be my best friend; the one always looking out for me and keeping me and others busy. He's a skinny guy with light freckles scattering his face. He doesn't like to miss deadlines or work. It's also kinda funny that his first name and my last name, Conrack, are pretty much alike.

Mike and Roger are like brothers, inseparable. Mike, the dark-brown haired and darker skinned man, loves to mess around. He makes fun of others, especially during lunch, and gets under people's skin a lot of the time. Roger, the shorter and more pale-skinned man, is a very active person. He just can't sit still and acts like a puppy who wants to play around all day.

Connor gets unbelievably annoyed by them. Since he is the bossy one of the group, he tries yelling and getting the two maniacs to calm down and prioritize the work. In the end, they do their job well. They're just a handful to deal with. Such as the time when Mike challenged Roger to a sword fight with metal poles.

They mainly work in the manufacturing part of the pipeline and make the signature blades for the bounty hunters. Since I'm the one around them while I pump the gas and pack in the coal for the furnaces, I know a thing or two. The blades are hidden and retract into the sleeves of the jackets. There are two blades, one on the top, and one at the bottom of the same wrist. The hunter reveals them when they take their thumb to the handle near the palm of the hand. They pull it up, and the blades come out.

On this particular day after refueling furnaces, unclogging pipes, and providing maintenance throughout the building, I go to the cafeteria, which is located on the first floor in the center of the building. The cafeteria is filled with tables that are lined symmetrically throughout the room.

I go to sit down at my table, which is near the entrance, with my pals Connor, Mike, and Roger. As I sit down, Connor starts by saying, "Hey, how was refueling?"

I answered with, "Eh, nothing much happened. Someone almost cut their hand but that was it," in an apathetic tone.

Mike notices my unenthusiastic mood and chimes in, "You guys know what will cheer this guy up?"

"Oh, I know. She'll be here any second. That'll get him going," Roger adds in and starts chuckling with Mike.

"Hey man, give the guy a break. He's been working hard. Still needs a minute or two to talk to her," laughs Connor.

"Ha ha, very funny guys. Really helps me," I say to the giggling goblins sitting next to me that I call my friends.

"We're just pulling your strings, bud. Have a little fun. We'll be out of here in no time, just a few more hours of work and then we're off for the day," says Connor as he pats me on the back.

Suddenly, everything starts to move in slow motion as a beautiful, dark-haired girl wearing bell-bottom jeans, grey work shirt, and a blue bandana headband walks in. Her name is Linda. She works in the communications portion of the building which is upstairs, so I don't get to see her that much.

She became part of our little friend group a few years ago and ever since we met her in this very large cafeteria, I still have never gotten the courage to ask her out. I've talked to her, and we both have some common interests—skiing, cooking, ice cream. I just haven't asked her to do any of those things with her. It makes my heart skip a beat every time I think about asking her.

As she is getting her food, Mike and Roger immediately start to tease me, making kissing noises just to mess with me. I blurt out, "Shut up! Why do you have to do this?"

"Cause it's what we do," they both say at the same time.

They stop with the noises when Linda sits down right next to me. Butterflies are flying in my stomach. Mike and Roger can barely hold in their laughter as they see my face go red. She asks, "What's so funny?" and chuckles to herself.

Mike and Roger manage to calm down a little, and Roger replies, "Oh nothing, just something he told me that was funny."

Connor nudges me on my left, clearing his throat and gesturing with his head to get me to tell her how I feel. As if he didn't give me enough signals. I shake my head. No way. I am still too nervous. Connor pulls out a long sigh, turns to Linda, and says, "They're laughing because he likes you." He points directly at me.

I look at my best friend dead in the eye making a face that tells him, what are you doing?! He smiles and continues, "He's had a crush on you for a while and is just too afr-"

"Ok, ok, I think you've said enough, buddy!" I interrupt before he finishes the sentence. I then hide part of my face from Linda and say, "I'm sorry you had to hear that, especially from him. He's crazy," I say, nervous and embarrassed.

"So then you *don't* have a crush on me after all this time we've been hanging out together?" Linda says.

I don't really catch it and start stuttering, "Well . . . that's not . . .  wh-what I meant... I mean, I do... you're v-very pretty." She starts smiling as I stutter and all I can muster is, "Sorry."

She puts her hand on mine and says, "Don't be nervous. It's not like I'm going to hit you or anything. When you're ready, you can tell me what you need to say." Her voice is kind and calm.

I can hardly say any more and have to take a deep breath to prevent myself from passing out. I look over to my other friends who are staring at me and smiling. I mouth the words "shut up" to them and start to smile at myself. All three of them continue to smile and shake their heads telling me that they won't stop.

I turn to Linda, who continues to eat her beef and broccoli. I start to collect my thoughts, but then suddenly my name is called. I look up to the entrance of the cafeteria and standing there is councilman Robins.

# ROBINS

A cold wind sweeps through the air, and it carries the smell of gas. It's a grey day, with hardly any sunlight. My hands, on the rail of the balcony, begin to stiffen, but I don't move them. The view before me is magnificent enough to distract me from the cold. I can see the growing and busy town in front of me as people start setting up a market on the sides of the roads. The roads are filled with cars, bikes and people walking across that pass countless buildings. The trees spread out vastly throughout the untouched areas up through the mountains.

I've watched the town grow for a long time, forty or so years, and my life here has taken a toll on me. For the last fourteen years, I've served on the council. There are five of us who have to take charge in one significant portion of the Academy. Charles Witemore watches over the pipeline and manufacturing, making sure utilities, weapon crafting, and automobile production goes swiftly. Robin Seth is in charge of communications and identification of any bounties. George Veisan handles the law enforcement and security of the Academy to ensure the safety of the workers. I'm in charge of bounty operatives and detainment. I'm the one who makes sure that bounties are clarified, captured, and paid for. Finally, there is the head councilman, Matthew Vanderbelt, who sets up recruitment and runs most of the Academy.

This job isn't easy, never has been, and I've been doing this for years as a hunter myself. I hate the idea of it, despise it, really, after the last few years, but I can't do anything about it since I am bound to the Academy and the workers. The Academy is not what it seems. I know that hunters choose to kill their bounties instead of detaining them. The entire purpose of the Academy is to track down assailants that walk the area and detain them, only killing them if necessary. But the Academy has changed in the last few years, and it's not clear to me why. All I know is that I want it gone.

I cannot sleep with the thought of this facility still running. This force has been corrupted, people need a chance to explain themselves, and I need to do something about it. But up until now, my condition has kept me from being able to figure out a way.

As I look up at the mountains now, I can't help but to think of the hunting and the killing. My best friend—the only one who ever understood me as a person—was also murdered. Her name was Laura, and she always stood by my side in order to calm my disorder down. Ever since the day of her death, it has become worse. My particular disorder is that I get angry at everything, not realizing I'm making decisions I wouldn't normally make, and this causes me to harm people or destroy objects that are near me.

I stare at the blanket of snow across the mountains, thinking of Laura, and I feel my rage building. My hands crumple into fists, and my knuckles grow white. My teeth are gritting, and before I know it, I start pounding on the metal rail of the balcony.

I storm back into the building. As I make for the stairs that lead back down to the first floor, I try my hardest to avoid eye contact with other people. It's like my body has a mind of its own. I couldn't control smashing my fists into the railing or onto the walls around me, and I needed to avoid people. By the time I get to the bottom of the stairs facing the auditorium, I turn to the corner behind me and attempt to breathe and calm down. No matter how hard I try, I feel the anger building up even more. Heat rises into my face, there's a loud pulsing in my eardrums, I grit my teeth.

My legs eventually take me to the back door of the pipeline.

I go past the cafeteria that sits in the middle behind the stairs and move directly to the back door. I can't explain the sense of fury I feel. I clench the knob as hard as my body can, and as I open the door, I feel like breaking it down. I stop to look into the room, a vein bulging in my forehead.

People are on break and eating, so no one is working. My eyes dart toward the long pipes running from left to right, both up to the other utilities and down to the furnaces. The propane tanks and furnaces catch my attention, and my brain starts to come up with a plan, one that I will not be proud of.

I want to blow the entire facility sky high, without a care for anyone inside. If I open the gas valves without setting off an alarm as well as take out any propane tanks along with opening the furnaces, the fire from the furnaces will catch and the whole thing will come down in seconds.

At this moment, my mind is speeding through this plan, going through every detail. I know that I will need more people to do this with me. A councilman entering a room he is not commanding would be suspicious. This job must be done with at least two people, and there is at least one person that I know of who I can get for this. That's David Conrack, Laura's son.

David doesn't know me that well, considering I never really spent time with him. Laura introduced me, but I was always nervous. The most time I got to spend time with him was introducing him to the Academy and showing him how to start his first job with his father.

However, he is the only other person working in the pipeline that I know of. While my angry mind is still flaring, I know I must find him and convince him to work with me in taking this corrupt organization down. But I have to be cautious about how I go about it. I can't tell him that I need to blow up the building just because I think the Academy is horrid. David is too loyal and will probably tell people about this big plan, so I have to bend the truth in order to get the job done. I'll just ask him if he can help me with refueling and taking out extra propane tanks to get the job done quicker.

As I am formulating my plan, I go back to the front entrance of the cafeteria. People are going in and out, and I try to breathe more in order to prevent myself from screaming or hitting something or someone. I open and close my hands a little to try to reduce the amount of pressure that causes my palms to throb. When I can, I enter the cafeteria again and look around for the dirty-blond, slightly curly-haired young man.

I scan the room until I see him sitting in between a skinny boy and a beautiful girl. I continue inside the cafeteria and say in as calm a voice as I can, "David." He looks up, almost scared to see me. "Can you come with me to my office, please? I need a favor from you," I say. I know I sound angry and irritated, and I hope he hasn't picked up on it.

He immediately stands up and comes over, following me towards the stairs without question. I look over to the auditorium where most meetings, trials, and executions take place. Just seeing this makes my face grow red with vexation. I keep my face turned away from David's, so he can't see the irritation building up in my eyes.

We reach the second floor with the corridors for the

dormitories, bathrooms, and offices. The offices are in the back part of the floor, past the dorms, which are lined up against the perimeter of the building opposite the bathrooms. The dorm rooms at the Academy are for anyone who does not have a home and mainly works here most of the time.

The voices from the cafeteria start to fade as we walk further down the hallways. We go past the door to the balcony on the left, and the hallway opens a bit more, revealing the five offices, one for each of the councilmen. The councilman's names are imprinted on the dark wooden door frames. I lead David to my office.

I struggle a bit with unlocking my office with my key, and when I finally succeed, I walk in quickly, instructing him, "Close the door behind you." My room is small, separated halfway by a curtain that blocks the view of my cot and dresser. Directly to the left is a desk covered with papers and documents and a lamp I'd left on, and behind the desk is my bookshelf. Most of the room is dimly lit by the one lamp on my desk. I see David take all this in.

I walk around to my chair and sit down, still opening and closing my hands, flexing my knuckles. With the door closed, I tell him, "I have a task for you that I can only reveal to you. You are the only person I can trust."

# DAVID

ooking into the eyes of this stringy-haired old man was like staring into the eyes of an angry serpent. The greenish blue pupils pierce through my soul as I stand there motionless listening to what task he has to offer. Even though I have known him for some time, but not really spending time together, he still gives a chilling presence. He's always been someone I was cautious about, especially now. His hands moved quite a bit and he gave some sort of an evil look.

"I need for you to take out more propane tanks and set them aside next to the stations around the workers and the furnaces. There is more demand in manufacturing the blades and other materials and we need them fairly quickly. There will be a rush tomorrow and I need you to get the propane from the storage. That's all I need," Robins says.

I'm a little confused about this, for two reasons. One, is that I never heard about a rush for manufacturing from anyone and especially not our councilman which is Councilman Witemore. Two, is that Councilman Robins shouldn't be the one asking me this favor, it should be Witemore. The task itself didn't sound difficult, it's the short notice that worried me. While thinking about this I say, "With all due respect councilman, but shouldn't Councilman Witemore tell us about this?"

As soon as I finished my question that I had the audacity to say, I immediately become terrified as Robins clenches his fist on the table and bit his lip. I shiver and flinch thinking that Robins might hit me. He looks at me and says, "Witemore is out for the day and asked me to tell the workers starting with you because it shouldn't be a hard job."

Now that I think about it, I didn't see Witemore at all today. I could've sworn that I saw him. Although, I am afraid to ask any more questions because Robins seems to want to break something in a couple seconds. In that case, all I can muster is, "Yes, sir. When would you like me to get started?"

"Tomorrow morning, six o'clock. Do not mention this to anyone," he said quickly.

I nod nervously and proceed to open the door to walk back

to my friends. I swear I can hear him knock something over or break an object as soon as I walk away from the door. My adrenaline starts to kick in as I begin to walk faster trying to get as far away from the room as possible.

I breeze through the hallways as if I was a car running on the highway. I almost lose my footing walking down the stairs and back to the cafeteria where my friends are waiting patiently for work to get started again.

They all look up at me as I walk towards my seat. Connor then says, "You alright? You look like you just saw a ghost."

"Was the old man that scary? Or did he turn into that ghost?" Mike chuckles.

I don't know what to say, for a moment I was speechless because I thought my head was gonna be torn off by the man that has been trained to do so for years. Not a word could come out of my mouth. I just stand there, face paralyzed just staring into the faces of my friends.

Then Linda grabs my hand and asks, "What did he ask you to do?" Somehow she is able to break me out of my trance, and I start to collect my thoughts. All I could think about was the anger behind those serpent-like eyes and the ominous task he has asked me to do.

"It's nothing really. He just asked me to get more fuel in the morning. I guess I just got a little nervous," I replied.

"Councilman Robins asked you to get more fuel? What about Witemore?" Connor asked, his eyebrows narrowing.

"He said Witemore was out today and tomorrow."

Connor, even more confused, looks at his comrades,

searching for help from them. Mike and Roger shrugged their shoulders not knowing what schedule Witemore had. Connor sighed and said, "I guess it's not that much of a job. I mean it's just pulling out cans of gas, right?"

I nodded and then he says, "Then you shouldn't have anything to worry about." Everyone at the table nods in agreement.

Something about the situation still worries me. Something about that terrifying stare of the experienced hunter made my skin crawl. I have never been more scared about something in my life. Typically, Robins was a twitchy person who has been said to hold a lot of anger. But this was like waiting for a volcano to erupt. I could feel the burning sensation of lava built up in his system.

Everyone starts getting up to go back to their stations. Linda grabs my hand once again to comfort me. Her hand felt like a soft blanket brushing across my palm. She made a smile that causes butterflies to scramble in my stomach. Everything about her made me forget what I was feeling moments ago. I was hoping that this feeling would last throughout the day and the next. The morning was not going to be pleasant, I could tell.

The morning became gloomy and grey with a cool air with no breeze. The mountain tops in the distance disappeared into the clouds that hung low covering some of the trees as well. Walking down the stairs from my dorm in silence was a little ominous.

Standing in front of the double-doored entrance are two figures. Robins, of course, waits impatiently shuffling his feet with his hands behind his back. Next to him is a short, dirty-blond boy who looks to be around thirteen. He has his head down as if he was nervous about something or rather he was reluctant to accomplish a task.

"Ah, good. You made it. I was afraid you had forgotten," Robins said, surprisingly calmly. "This is Vance, one of the boys that works on the electricity. He will be helping with transferring more fuel to the furnaces."

I look at Vance and nod, trying to muster a "hello". He gives a small, nervous wave and looks back down at his feet. The awkward greeting was then silenced by Robins, "Now you boys know your jobs, correct?" He looked at me, and I nodded in understanding. Then he looked at Vance searching for an acknowledgment from the boy, but the teenager just stared at his feet, and Robins began to glare at him with intensity, "Correct?" he said in a louder tone. Vance jumped and immediately nodded several times saying, "Yes, sir. Er . . . Councilman."

Vance looked really scared, which intensified my own sense of fear. What concerns me is how Robins got Vance to do this job in the first place and what Vance's job is supposed to be. Nothing about this job felt right, not even a little bit. I so badly wanted to refuse this job, but something told me that I had to do what he said. His gaze gave a sense that he might do something awful to one of us if not both. So I decided to stay silent.

"Alright, let's get this over with," he said. "I'll be upstairs if you need anything." Then he opened the door and we walked inside. The facility isn't very busy. Only a small portion of the workers work the night and early morning shift. The need to do so was never really necessary considering most of the hunting work is done during the day. The building was quite silent, every once and a while we could hear the footsteps of people upstairs.

Me and Vance walk into the pipeline and I don't know what to say to make him feel better. The boy is shaking with fear, holding his arms in his stomach looking like he might vomit. "Everything alright?" I finally said.

Vance looked at me for a second and then looked down again and said, "No not really."

"What's wrong?" I said.

"Councilman Robins was saying that I better not mess up the gas or something bad will happen to me."

I took a second to think of a response as I didn't know what to say or how to make him feel better. All I can say is, "You won't mess it up," as he started to go left towards the power box and I went right towards the fuel storage.

Opening the storage door reveals a large room full of tanks the size of a small tire to the size of tables. Some stand on shelves along the walls while the larger tanks sit in the middle of the room. Along the shelves consists of other parts for any of the blades we made or even automobile parts for the other building behind the Academy. That building was for the car building, but I've never been there myself.

I start grabbing one tank at a time from the shelves and

carry them to each station lined up in front of the furnaces next to the blow torches. One by one each station is prepped with at least two more tanks ready for the torches. The storage starts to dwindle in the fuel tanks from the shelves as my muscles begin to ache.

All of a sudden the alarm bell goes off with a piercing ringing noise. I jumped, startled at what was happening. I look around towards the power and gas pipes where Vance is standing terrified and holding his head. He stares at the wide open gas pipe that seems to be spewing out fuel. Everyone in the room yelled in confusion and anger and began to scramble out of the pipeline.

I sprint to the poor boy who seems to be paralyzed, "What the hell happened? Why is the pipe open?" I yell.

"I . . . I . . . I guess I didn't turn off the alarm," he says.

"Why would you need to turn off the alarm? Especially if you are transferring gas. And why did you open it?"

"That's what Councilman Robins said. But I didn't know what to do with gas because I haven't learned all of it yet."

Immediately I turn to the gas valve on the pipe and switch it off in order to prevent more gas from flowing in. "We need to get out of here, now!" I said.

Vance and I quickly ran down the hallways leading to the entrance of the building with the sound of the alarm still ringing throughout the block. More people from the dorms and classrooms hurry for the exit, screaming and yelling curse words. We push open the doors outside to the cool air and a grey sky still blankets over the town. All of the people congregate on the other side of the street gape as Vance and I burst out of the facility.

One man from the group, full brown bearded and fairly built, pointed at us and yelled, "They were the ones on the pipes!"

# 4

## DAVID

Complete panic and adrenaline built up in my system, not knowing what to do. The crowd began to rile up in anger, holding up fists and pointing fingers. My eyes dart from person to person as I do my best to collect my words, but nothing comes out of my mouth. Each accusation that a person threw at us was like a punch to our throats, preventing any noise from coming out.

I turn to Vance standing to my left and he is shaking in fear. The tears well up in his eyes and start rolling down his face. His lips quivered and his face turned bright red. I didn't know what to do. There is nothing we can say to this angry mob, nothing that could go over the sound of their yelling.

I tried defending our case saying that we were trying to stop the leak, but no one could hear over their own screaming. I started looking around to see if anyone would be able to help us and stop on my right. Standing there with fists clenched with white knuckles was Robins. His gaze petrified me, he looked like he was about to charge. I didn't think he would actually do it, until he started running in our direction. I thought he was coming for me, so I began walking backward and sprinting for my life. But he wasn't going for me, he wanted Vance.

The kid barely sees the giant, angry man lunging at him with incredible speed for his age and nearly grabs him as he drops to the ground. Vance desperately crawls away from Robins. He whimpers while the staggered councilman continues to charge at him.

I feel a rush coursing through my veins, the blood pumps even faster. I had to do something in order to help Vance, Robins will do something horrible if I don't. Then, before I know it, I sprint towards Vance. I shot off like a bullet, using every drop of energy I have in order to reach Vance before Robins could.

Robins is nearly there and reaches for the crying boy. I decide to change directions and ram straight into the raging councilman. The impact surprises Robins and causes me to stagger to the ground as well. Both of us tumble onto the rough concrete.

A burning sensation appeared on my right arm where a scrape from the sidewalk formed. I shake it off as I get up and look at Vance's attacker who is getting up off the ground. The string-haired man gazed upon me, his eyebrows moved closer together and his teeth gritted.

As I backed away from Robins, a heavy force pushed me to the ground. The police of the area pinned me and Vance to the ground before Robins could do anything. The cuffs tightened around my wrists and I was immediately picked up by the two officers beside me.

The officers drag me away from the scene and past the loud crowd of people. I could hear people in the group shout out things like, "Hope you rot in hell!" or "Execute them!" The anger of the crowd could be heard for many blocks. People in cars driving by give confused looks out their window as they try to make out what was going on.

The officers put me in the back seat of the police car and I began to panic. My thoughts rambled. *What's going to happen to me? Are they going to execute me? Will I be behind bars for the rest of my life for something I didn't do?* All I know is that I was about to be held in a cell before they put me in trial at the Academy.

I look back out the window to the still screaming group of workers. To the right of them is Robins, staring at me with a vein popping out on his face. I couldn't look away as if he took me into a trance. Just as the car starts to move, he makes a gesture with his thumb sliding across his throat. Indicating that he wants me dead.

The fear sunk in, and I could barely breathe. I wanted to say something to the officers that would convince them that Vance and I were innocent. I began to gather my thoughts and do my best to talk to them.

"Officers, please, you have to believe that we didn't try doing anything to harm anyone. We were trying to patch up and stop the gas pipe," I said.

The driver scorned, "That's what every criminal says when people hear something about sabotaging the Academy." He has a deep, raspy voice and a thick, black beard.

"Please listen, Councilman Robins was behind this. He's the one that wants the Academy gone," I said as my heart races even more.

The officer in the passenger seat laughed, "You're blaming the councilman? One of the people that keeps the place alive and swears an oath to it? Your story just becomes less and less believable." He has a higher voice and a younger face. He looked fairly new to the enforcement.

"Besides, we hear that a lot, too. People blaming councilmen, mainly Robins. You're not the first one, kid. You're not getting out of this one," the driver said.

"He's not what you think. He threatened the boy who is thirteen in the other car that you guys arrested. He chased him like he was going to kill him. You can't tell me that something is wrong with him," I said, my eyes welling up.

The officers gave a glance to one another, but didn't say a word after that. I figure there is no point in trying to convince them after that thought. They still drive towards the station, which isn't too far from the Academy. We take a few turns towards a more country part of town, away from most of the large structures. The building I was gonna be locked up in was a large, flat "L" shape with the bottom part of the "L" protruding toward us on the left. We stop at the entrance to the right, the officers quickly get out of the car simultaneously, and proceed to drag me out of the car and into the station.

I can't believe that any of this is happening. A part of me is thinking that this is all a dream. I want it all to be over but I know it isn't yet.

Walking in, the room is lined with work desks which one was hardly occupied. Each one filled with paper documents, decorations like ornaments and plants, and mugs. One officer looked up at me as he was going through his documents and laughed, shook his head and looked back at his papers.

I feel agitated, anxious, horrified, I didn't want to be here. My heart drops as we turn the corner to the left towards the cell block. It is cold, the smell of sweat burned through my nostrils. It is a long hallway, partially filled with inmates. There is a room towards the back that I couldn't see clearly. It's too far away and too dark in the room for me to be able to see it.

The officer holding me, the raspy voiced one, opened a cell to the right and shoved me in. Inside, it is small and depressing and ever so timid. Nothing stood here except a bunk against the wall and a toilet to the right. A very small and rectangular window sat above the bunk close to the ceiling.

I turn around as the clanking of the iron bars is sealed shut. I stare up at the officer and say, "Please think about it." He said nothing and looked down as he started walking away towards the lobby.

"David? David?!" an anxious voice echoes from the cell next to me.

"Vance? Are you alright?" I answer.

"What's going to happen to us? Are we going to be here forever?"

"Everything is going to be alright," I said lying, trying to keep him calm. I have no idea what is to come. I don't know if we are going to be behind bars for the rest of our lives, have ourselves killed, or magically be let go to do our normal daily routine. I highly doubt that would happen but a man can dream.

In a situation like this, when a person in the Academy gets convicted of a crime they are put on trial at the facility in the auditorium. The government doesn't support our program and pays no attention to it. Therefore, we run it in our own ways. The councilmen discuss the sentence for that person and are either killed in front of the audience, put in jail, or very rarely let go.

"David?" Vance asked.

"Yeah man?" I answered.

"Why did Councilman Robins want me to turn off the alarm?"

"Because he didn't want people to know, I guess," I exclaimed.

"But why? Why would he do that?" he questioned.

As Vance was asking the question, the realization began to strike me. If Robins told Vance to open the gas valve and turn off the alarm while the furnaces were on, not to mention the extra can of propane that I hauled out, that means there was only one solution, "Because Robins was going to blow up the whole Academy."

The hours fly by as I lie down on the surprisingly comfortable bunk. I don't exactly know how much time has passed since all I have been doing was staring up at the ceiling. Vance was taken away a while ago for his own trial, I imagine I'll be next soon. The only thing that I can do is hope that they let Vance go. After all, he's just a kid.

Everything was still, no sound was coming from the corridor, the lobby, or even outside. I swear I could almost hear the daylight radiating through the small window above me. Silence filled the building, not even the inmates there were talking.

Finally, the silence is broken very suddenly. The sound of steps scrambled from the back of the building. The rattle of keys sounds and I get up to see what is going on. I sit up on my bunk and I can hear grunting and coughing. What came in my line of sight is the raspy voiced officer. But what startles me is that he is covered in blood. He struggles to stand and grabs the iron bar gate, he is holding his stomach as if his insides were about to fall out which is where he is bleeding profusely.

He began to unlock the door and he said in a gargled voice this time, "You . . . were . . . right." My eyes widened, I thought I was having a nightmare. I couldn't believe anything about what was happening.

The officer pulled the gate open with all his strength that he had left and laid there motionless. My heart is pounding, I could feel my veins pumping faster and the blood rushing throughout my body. The adrenaline kicked in and my instincts tell me I have to get out of here.

I couldn't go through the front door, they'll think that I murdered the officer is what I thought. I have to go through the back as quickly as I can. I'm not thinking about much, only that I'm scared and that I need to get out of this building.

I start running towards the right to the bottom of the L, looking for a back exit. In seconds I was past the long corridor of cell blocks. I ran next to an open door that led to a dark room with blinking lights. I look inside and it looks to be some kind of a communications room that keeps in contact with the Academy. But this room is damaged. Toppled desks, chairs, and papers all around the floor. One desk was up right with the body of another officer lying on top of it. It's the other officer that was in the passenger seat. Robins must have gotten to them because he knew that I was going to tell them that he wanted to destroy the Academy.

I sprint past the room and turn to the left down the bottom part of the L. It's a small hallway that consists of storage units, bathrooms, and a breakroom. I didn't care or pay much attention to the other rooms. All I looked for was an exit which was straight ahead. I opened the door, practically bursting through it and headed towards the Academy.

I thought maybe if I get one of the other councilmen then maybe they would help me. Maybe Councilman Witemore will help me, he's watched over me for a while. I should get my friends too, Connor, Linda, they'll understand that I wasn't behind all this.

First thing's first is I have to get there. So the running began once again and I followed the road back into the town. It's more luminescent outside than it was in the morning, the clouds have cleared up a bit more. The time might be close to noon judging by the positioning of the sun. So I might be able to catch up with my friends before their break ends.

I use as much energy as I can to run even faster, take a left, and directly ahead is the facility. Turning the corner I almost ran into an old man, spinning around him like a maniac and apologizing before continuing my marathon. Other people start crossing into the line of my dash and I slow down in order to dodge the people in the way. I turn my shoulders in order to scamper by without hitting them.

Eventually I'm left an open space for me to continue the dead sprint. My heart continues to pound, my head and back pours down with sweat and my legs feel weightless. My breath becomes short but I continue to press on as I did not think that the distance was going to be that long. But the building is in my sights. *I can make it,* I said to myself. So I press on, following the sidewalk.

I finally make it to the mansion-like structure and slow down to a trod to catch my breath. I look back to see if the police are following me and find nothing. I enter through the double doors to the Academy still breathing heavily to catch my breath.

Looking around I could see people walking out of the cafeteria, which means I just missed lunch. That also means that I could still catch my friends before they go back to work. My eyes darted around the group of workers to see if I could spot a pale, skinny man or a beautiful dark haired girl. I walk into the crowd in order to get a more thorough look, not having much luck.

I look towards the entrance to the pipeline and there I see Connor talking to Mike and Roger to the side as people walk in, thankful that nothing happened to them. I push through everyone to get there, practically scraping against the wall to get past everyone. I managed to squeeze through and yelled out, "Connor!" as I interrupted their conversation.

A puzzled and surprised expression grew on my best friend's

face, "David? How are you here right now? You're supposed to be in a cell right now."

"Listen, you have to believe me. I didn't do anything that Robins says, I assume you guys heard it all," I said.

Mike answered, "We heard, alright. We started questioning it ourselves. We didn't think you'd actually blow the place up."

I sighed in relief, "Good, because I need to talk to Councilman Witemore so that-"

Roger cut me off, "That'll be tough."

"Why?" I said, my heart dropping below sea level.

Connor gave a worried look at me, "They placed a bounty on you, David. Which is why you need to get out of here right now," he said in a lower tone.

Now I was terrified and paranoid, I looked around to see if people noticed me.

Connor continued, "They did it not too long ago, Linda got word that you killed a few officers at the station."

I can't believe what is happening, Robins is making everyone turn on me for something that he did. Now I'm wanted, dead or alive probably. I'm speechless, I don't know what to say because of how scared I am.

Mike pulls out a piece of paper and hands it to me and says, "You don't have much time. Go into the market in town and find a place with those words and numbers."

I looked at the note that wrote, *Weiland Harrison 4444 5555.* "What place is this? What do the numbers mean?" I asked, panicking.

But Connor gestures that I need to go now. He looked to the

right of me which looked like a hunter staring at us. It's hard to see what he looked like without the light. All I know is that he is big. I looked back at my friends who I consider my family and said, "Thank you," as I turned away and ran for the exit.

As I leave the Academy, my vision becomes blurry as tears well up and roll down my face in the thought that I may never see my friends again. I may even die trying to escape this nightmare. My friends might die because they helped me. All these thoughts made the tears run down my face even more. But I know that there is no turning back now, my friends did that so that I may live and escape.

Mike said to go to the market in town, so that's exactly where I'm gonna go. The hunters are behind me so I have to make as much distance as I can. Once again, the sprinting continued heading towards the clump of structures. I do not look back, afraid that the hunters are about to catch me.

The market up ahead was full of goods, fruits, candy, clothing and jewelry. Some pavilions are set up to provide shade and some of the shops around town are open. Large groups of people are gathered here, which will make it hard to run and search for whatever the note is telling me.

I opened the note once again to remember what I was looking for. The problem is that I don't know what the numbers mean. I'm searching around looking for signs that could possibly say the names Weiland or Harrison. Pavilion after pavilion I continue to frantically search for some indication of the words or the numbers. I'm shoving people out of the walkway, thinking that I might get caught soon by a hunter.

I look up at the buildings as well, hoping that one of the writings on the piece of paper would show up. Finally, to the left is a large clothing shop that has the name, *Weiland and Harrison Clothing* above the entrance door that hangs wide open. I don't hesitate and I dart straight into the shop.

This place is filled with racks of different types of clothing, shirts, polos, jeans, jackets and more sitting on wooden flooring. The space is larger than I thought, the ceiling stood high above me and a small staircase in the back led to a second floor. Paintings scattered the walls and a room sat at the back, probably for trying on the clothes. There is another part of the building towards the left that I couldn't see clearly. A chandelier hung in the center of the ceiling halfway down the building.

A boy is sitting on a chair to the right, reading the newspaper wearing an Irish hat. As I walked in, he looked up and said, "Hello, sir. What can I do for ya?" he said with a big smile.

I quickly showed him the piece of paper hoping that he would understand, cause lord knows what the numbers mean. "Can you or someone here help me?" I asked desperately.

The cheerful expression on the kid's face slowly turned to a serious one. He nodded, got up out of the chair and ran to the left part of the building. I look back out at the market and there standing in a polo jacket is a hunter. He was looking down the streets so he hadn't seen me yet. I could tell he is a hunter because the hidden blade could be seen in his sleeve. That told me he was a bit sloppy, not keeping it hidden very well ironically.

I quickly go to the back of the shop towards the jackets in

the corner. I hide behind the rack hoping that they won't see me. I stare at the door waiting for the hunter to walk in, but he isn't the one to walk in. My heart rose up again and the world stopped spinning for a second as Linda walked in. I couldn't believe it, why is she all the way over here and how?

"Linda!" I said, revealing myself from the jackets.

She looks at me with sparkling eyes, "David!" and ran towards me wrapping her arms around in a big hug. "I'm so glad you're okay, but I need you to act like you're buying clothes cause the hunter is right outside."

I listen to her, turning my back towards the entrance and pretending to look for a jacket. The hunter must have come in when Linda swiftly chose a grey bomber jacket for me to put on. She whispered,"Don't look back, he's right there."

My heart skipped a beat when she said that. There is nowhere else to run, we are exposed. All we can do is hope that he didn't pay any attention to us. I could hear the steps on the wooden floors slowly walking closer to us. Linda took my hand, ensuring that everything will be alright.

Eventually, the steps got quieter and further away. The hunter had left. Me and Linda sighed in relief. "I thought I'd never see you again, how did you know where I was?" I asked.

I turned to her smiling and she answered, "I saw you run away from the Academy, I just had to come looking for you after they announced the bounty. There was no way I would let them take you. Why would they think you did all that?"

"It's Robins, he wanted us to leak gas into the pipeline and blow it up. He probably knew that I would tell the officers so he killed them."

Linda didn't look surprised, she seemed more angry than anything, "Why would he do such a thing?"

I shrugged, "I don't know, but none of that matters now that the bounty is on me. You shouldn't be here with me, you need to go. I don't want to put you in danger."

"No, I'm staying with you. I already committed to this and there's no going back," she said.

"Linda, I can't risk-" I was cut off by the sound of rocks moving. It was coming from behind me. I look back and a part of the wall has moved and a man is standing there and said, "Don't just stand there, lads. We gotta get movin'."

# ROBINS

My head is pounding, feeling like it's about to explode. My anger is still built up from this morning uncontrollably, but not as horribly. Although, enough to force me to want to get this trial done as fast as possible. I'm walking towards the stage of the auditorium where the other councilmen sit in their chairs with Vanderbelt in the middle.

The auditorium is a very open, echoey space with large arches covering the ceiling. Long benches stretch from left to right across the room much like a church facing the stage where every worker in the Academy is waiting for the trial of a thirteen year old boy. That boy stands to the side of the councilmen with a hunter holding his shoulder to prevent him from going anywhere.

My energy is slowly dying down which starts suppressing the anger fuming in my body as I walk up the steps to my seat right next to Vanderbelt. I hardly pay attention to anyone in the room as I hold my head which is throbbing in pain. I grunt as I sit down in my chair and before I knew it, Vanderbilt started the gathering.

"Ladies and gentleman, you all have been summoned here to discuss the crimes that have been committed by Vance Aimstrem. His actions threatened the lives of many people sitting here right now and threatened the Academy itself. He has been accused of attempting to obliterate the pipeline by opening a gas pipe and letting it leak. This was in cooperation with David Conrack who has now been placed under bounty and is now on the run. The accused is now allowed to plead."

The hunter holding Vance pushed him forward towards the center of the stage. Vance looked at me in betrayal and complete and utter fear. The tears poured down his face as he went up on stage. I wanted to say something, but the outcome would not be in my favor. I still want the Academy gone, I want it defeated in some way. That is why I need to be quiet about it. However, Vance was taking all the blame and it was my fault.

Vance started to talk, "I . . . I didn't do anything. I . . . I was trying to check for leaks," he continued to cry and his voice started to rise. "I . . . It was my first time doing the job," he stuttered. "I wasn't sure I knew what to do."

A man in the audience then rose up quickly in his seat and cursed at the boy, "I saw you and the other man messin' with them pipes! We all knew it was you, boy!" The rest of the crowd began to rile up and point at the sobbing boy, calling him names. The noise makes my head throb.

Vanderbelt grabs his gavel and crashes it against the hardwood to silence the crowd, which made my body twitch due to the surprise and close quarters. "It is clear that the witnesses and the evidence supports this claim of Vance Aimstrem. We all know the punishment for threatening the facility, and that is death by electric chair," Vanderbelt said.

My realization kicked in, my eyes widened and my head rose up. I turned to Vanderbelt and spoke softly and the crowd began to mutter, "Hold on, we're talking about executing a kid here. He's only thirteen, we can't do this," I said, trying not to seem too desperate.

"You should know the rules here, Steven. Those who threaten the Academy must be sentenced to death. Otherwise a criminal walks and the hunters and workers will not obey orders," Vanderbelt responded.

"But this is a kid, look at him. He is sobbing, he's distraught."

"That's what we want them to see, to have criminals regret their decisions. No second chances." He struck the hardwood twice, "Guilty, bring the chair."

I felt defeated, guilty, shocked. The councilmen began to leave the table as I stood there not believing what I just heard.

I swiftly get out of my chair and walk out of the auditorium. Not knowing where I would go, I got to a corner in the back of the building close to the pipeline area. My eyes begin to water as the moments sink in. I had just caused a thirteen year old boy to be executed by being electrocuted in front of a crowd. *What have I done? How would I fix this? Is it even possible to do so? My mind could not cope with this kind of guilt. What would Laura do?*

Suddenly someone came up behind me, "Sir, we are in pursuit of David Conrack. But he has hid in the market and we're starting to lose track of him," he says.

Perfect, not only did I have the execution to worry about but also David who is currently being hunted. I couldn't call off the bounty once it was placed, that's done. I had to do the standard routine in order to keep my secret hidden. David knew what I was doing and cannot have him risk blowing my cover. I have to make a decision.

I turned to the hunter, making sure my face showed no sign of grief and said, "Search the perimeter, surround the area to prevent his escape. He couldn't have gone too far." The hunter then nodded and walked away towards the auditorium.

As he disappears around the corner, my brain begins to crank. There has to be some way to save this boy. I cannot let them get away with the execution of a teenager who is innocent. But there isn't a way to get him out, hunters are holding him and preparing him for his death. If I were to break him out that would mean fighting through and exposing myself as the actual criminal. There's no way that I will be able to prevent Vance from being killed. That's it, the end of a short life, I thought.

Then a lightbulb lit up in my brain. An idea that will not prevent the execution, but will allow him to survive. It was a mad and risky idea, but it might work. The idea is to use an anesthetic to make it seem like Vance would be dead. If I could perform it well enough and make it convincing for both the audience and executioners, then I can save him. He would be able to walk free without anyone knowing he was alive.

I know one place where there is some anesthetic, the infirmary, which is in the back of the building and past the pipeline. The infirmary is mainly used for any hunters that were injured severely or even illnesses for workers in the Academy. There had to be something in there I could use, I have seen procedures being worked on hunters before and saved many lives. There has to be something, I know it.

I quickly walk into the more enclosed room full of cabinets, beds and medical supplies. The sterile smell engulfed the room, cloaking the gas smells coming from the pipeline. The beds are lined up on the right side of the wall and a curtain hung in the back. Opposite of the beds are the wall of cabinets holding a variety of tools and drugs. The items left there consisted of cotton balls, q-tips, bandages and gauze.

What gives me a sigh of relief is that the nurse was not here, of course because of the meeting and now the execution probably. I rapidly reach the cabinets and start opening the bottom ones. Bottles and machines sit here such as Alka-Seltzer and Aspirin. This first cabinet must be for minor illnesses. This search was gonna take a while I thought until I found something in one of the middle cabinets. It is a bottle of Ether, an anesthetic used to knock someone out in order to perform a procedure more efficiently. And next to it is Epinephrine, something I can use to wake up Vance once I drag him out. It was perfect, it would make Vance seem like he has passed to the audience and make an escape.

"Can I help you with something?" a voice said suddenly. It was the nurse entering the room. I jump in surprise, letting go of the bottle of ether and stand up. "

"I'm sorry for intruding, I was hoping to find something for a headache?" I said coming up with a fast excuse.

The blond-haired and beautiful nurse smiled, "Oh, well then I believe there is some bufferin in the cabinet to your left, sir."

I crouch once again to open the next cabinet and swiftly use a sleight of hand to grab the ether that is the size of my palm and place it in my jacket pocket along with the epinephrine with a syringe for both. The cabinet door is used as a cover to make sure she wouldn't see it. I grab the bufferin and stand up, "Ah, thank you very much." I open the bottle of tablets and pop one in my mouth. It was an excellent excuse since my head was hurting.

As soon as I put the bufferin back I close the cabinets and immediately start walking out of the infirmary, waving at the nurse goodbye as she places papers onto her desk.

This will determine whether I will save a young boy's life or cause the death of his and my own.

# 7

# ROBINS

veryone chats quietly throughout the auditorium, anxiously waiting for this execution to be done and over with. I tap my foot on the ground nervously while I wait for them to bring out Vance to the electric chair that has been set up. Typically, the electric chair is supposed to strap to the head while it has been wet down with a sponge. This one in particular straps around the neck, which still gives a similar effect but instead makes them feel like they are choking.

Finally, the hunter brings out Vance, who is now dressed in a white button down and dress pants to make him look presentable. As soon as he seats Vance into the chair, the tears immediately roll down his face once again as he realizes that this is the end of his early road.

I stand up to begin strapping Vance into his wired seat with the syringe of ether in my pocket. I start from the ankles, locking them in with straps much like a belt. The wrists are being locked next and then the neck band is placed over and around his throat. While I prepare the neck band I whisper, "It'll be alright, trust me and don't make a sound," in order to reassure him that this will not be his end.

Vance gives me a confused look as I bring out the syringe. With a sleight of hand, I pressed the needle into his arm in one swift moment. To my surprise, Vance didn't flinch nor mutter a sound. None of the crowd or the councilman said anything, which indicated that I was in the clear. I quickly slip the syringe in my sleeve and start walking away.

Vanderbelt starts announcing to the audience, "Vance Aimstrem, you have been condemned for threatening this facility and the people of the Academy and sentenced to death. Do you have anything to say before the sentence is carried out?"

Vance was shaking, "I . . . I'm sorry," is all he could mutter.

Vanderbelt looked at me and nodded for me to continue with the execution. I hesitated, fearing that this plan was not going to work. Although, what choice do I have but to go through with it now. I walk to the left of the auditorium towards the lever to activate the chair. I took hold of it, squinting and hoping that this plan would work.

Then, I pull it down, sending waves of electricity into the chair and through Vance's body. He jerked up with the straps holding him down, making a muffled scream as the band around the neck prevented him from letting out a full yelp. His muscles tensed and his body shook rapidly until suddenly, his body started to go limp after several minutes. I then pull the lever back up quickly stopping the charge.

Vance sat there motionless, not making a sound. The hunter holding him checked him, looking for a pulse on the wrist and even at the neck where it looked burnt red. He looked up at me and said, "He's gone," in a deep voice. "One electrocution seemed to be enough."

The audience seemed to speak amongst themselves, seeming skeptical that one electrocution was able to kill him. Usually the shock would go on longer and the typical execution would take two or three shocks.

"Do another shock just in case," Vanderbelt said to me.

I looked at him and my heart sank, "Like he said, it seemed to be enough. A boy could not survive that. There's no use electrocuting a dead corpse, just roll him out," I said.

Vanderbelt frowned and looked at the other councilman as if searching for assistance. He looked at me again and gave a wry smile, "Very well, Robins. You're the professional."

When it was done, Vance was presumed dead. Hopefully it's not true and the ether was able to do its job. My body shook, concerned that Vance might not be able to wake up. The room cleared as each person was now going back to their job.

The hunter brought a cart to move the body out and I gestured to him that I will do it myself. I unstrap Vance, revealing red marks on the skin. The neck is slightly burnt, bright red and blisters have started forming. I lifted him off the chair, laid him down on the cart, and rolled him towards the back of the stage.

Past the curtains is a disposal, a large garbage chute opening sat on the wall. Body bags and other carts are in here as well near the corners. Getting closer to the disposal always opened my nostrils to the overwhelming smell of death and decay. The bodies would later be burnt, but the place still wreaked of dead flesh.

I stop the cart, quickly look around and listen to make sure no one is around. Knowing that no one is here, I pull out a second syringe and the bottle of epinephrine. I loaded the syringe and injected the epinephrine into Vance's arm hoping for dear life that this would work.

After waiting a little bit, nothing happened. Vance still laid there motionless, no breathing. I failed, I just let a little boy die because of my own uncontrollable condition. My body felt weak and weightless. Until suddenly, Vance rose up like a bullet leaving the barrel of a gun. He is gasping for air but the injury to his neck is causing him to take in short breaths.

"Calm down, calm down. It's alright, breathe through your nose!" I said. It takes no time for him to listen and start moving air in and out through his nostrils. "Look, you need to be quiet, alright? The whole place believes you're dead. This will be your chance to live somewhere else, somewhere away from his hell hole."

He tried talking, but his voice was so muffled I could barely understand. "Why . . . are . . . you . . . helping?" he finally said.

I put my head down as I finally understood what he said, collecting my thoughts. I brought my head back up and said, "I'm so, so so sorry, kid," with tears welling up in my eyes. "I couldn't let you die because of something that I did. My anger . . . I just can't control it sometimes. But now you can leave and no one will notice. And we need to keep it that way."

Vance nods in understanding and starts to get up off the cart. "Careful, son," I say and help him on his feet. His legs wobble under him but are still able to keep him standing. I continue to help him walk and we head towards a back door on the left side of the auditorium just past the curtains. I stop before we get in sight.

"Alright, now you have to be careful, hunters are out there and they will be able to recognize you," I warned him. I pull out a small handful of dollar bills and hand it to him, "This will get you food and any supplies and possibly a place to sleep." I then roll up my right sleeve where my hidden blades are and start unstrapping it.

The blades take up the forearm and are strapped at the front and back and a handle is right under the thumb in order to release the two blades that are on the top above the knuckles and the bottom below the palm. I take the whole thing off and hand it to Vance. "Just slip this in on the way and get as far away from here as possible. Get to the mountains if you have to. Use this blade if you have to, only to protect yourself. Pull the handle with your thumb in order to activate it."

Vance looks up at me with the eyes of a dog and says, "Thank you," in a soft but in a much less damaged voice.

I look to see if anyone is looking in our direction and luckily there is hardly anyone around. I walk towards the exit and gesture to Vance with my hand to come towards him and open the door. Before I knew it, Vance was gone and out of the building. The relief flowed through my body, the plan had worked.

# ROBINS

I feel weightless as I walk away from the back door towards the stairs. Knowing that no one knew that Vance escaped, much less survived, sent a wave of comfort and calm. However, that started to change when a woman came towards me and said, "Councilman, you are needed in communications."

I quickly change directions towards the back next to the infirmary. The room is smaller and more enclosed. Radars, screens and generators fill the sides of the room, making it feel more claustrophobic. Four people sit in this room, a couple of them wearing headphones to listen to the ones in vehicles and in the field.

One man wearing headphones turned to me and took them off, "David has disappeared within the crowd at the market, we're unsure of his whereabouts," he said.

Now there is another problem, just when I thought I was doing well after I helped Vance. But now David is on the run, and that's my fault too. My rage caused the death of those officers to make sure no one knew about my intentions. David is the main source of that, and although I didn't want him hurt I still cannot reveal myself. Even if I want to help him there is nothing I can do, the bounty is already set and cannot be lifted or changed. He's wanted dead or alive.

I have to give orders to keep my cover. "He couldn't have gone far. Send out the Sweepers, circle the town. If he's gone farther than we thought we'll catch him with the Sweepers," I said.

Sweepers are our uniquely built cars, designed to be fast and durable. They can turn through tight corners and run on difficult terrain such as thick forests and rocky, mountainous areas. They even run on water and act as a boat. The vehicle is bullet proof, even the windows cannot be broken down easily. Each car comes with its own password on a keypad that only the driver knows. Anything done to the keypad or an attempt to hotwire it will shut down the car completely. These vehicles are designed to catch their bounties indefinitely. So few have escaped them and lived.

I did not want to suggest these but it was my standard routine whenever a bounty starts making their escape. The people on the headset started making their announcements to unleash the Sweepers. At that moment, a woman on the screen asked, "Sir, do you think David has made contact with the other Runaways?"

She meant the runaways from before, many people have disbelieved the Academy before and attempted escaping like David and even tried plotting against it like me. Some have never been found, which makes us believe that there is a place they are staying hidden in. That's what she was talking about.

"Let's hope not, I don't want another Runaway on the loose," I said.

Come to think of it, that's exactly what I want. Not only would I want David to escape, but to also get with the other Runaways if they are all together. Even if that is only a rumor, I could only hope that it would be true.

# 9

## DAVID

The man guiding us to this hidden door is old, around his sixties or maybe seventies. His hair is grey and took the shape of his head as it laid flat. He wore a duffle coat and carried a lantern. As we passed the entrance, the door slid shut and he turned to us.

"Howdy, name's Roy, and boy are y'all lucky!" he said in a southern accent.

"Thank you so much! How can we thank you?" Linda said in relief.

"Y'all can thank me once ya' get to safety," he responded and gestured toward the rest of the tunnel.

Linda and I start walking down this dark and eerie tunnel. The smell of dirt engulfed the enclosed area. The width of the tunnel is small, just enough for one person at a time to walk without touching the wall. I led the party with Linda directly behind me and Roy walked in the back.

A staircase led us downward to a light after a minute of walking in silence. The exit opened under a bridge where a railroad sat in the middle facing perpendicular to where we came out of the tunnel. Towards the sides of the railroad tracks is dense forest, tall and green trees shook subtly in the light breeze.

"We should be safe here fer now," Roy said, "Them Rippers won't find that passage. They should be lookin' deep in the town now. Y'all aren't the first ones through there."

"Rippers?" I asked not ever hearing the term before.

"Rippers, hunters, it's what we call 'em. 'Cause of their blades and all," Roy explained. "They're pro'ly gonna head to the woods soon, better get movin'."

We start moving past the bridge, walking parallel with the tracks. It was silent, hardly anything moved out here. The only movement is from the trees in the wind. The sounds of birds are chirping, the only sound I could hear besides our steps in the grass.

"Y'all need to get to them mountains before the Rippers get to ya. There'll be a camp there ya can get to. I can help ya get to the forest before the track turns, but I have to get back to be with my grandson," Roy explained.

"It really means a lot that you came all this way to help us," I said with appreciation. "How many people are at this camp?"

"Not a whole lot, twenty maybe," Roy answered.

"How many tried to escape?" Linda asked.

"Too many ta count. Rippers are hard to get away from, ya know? Dozens have tried, few made it."

My heart sunk on that answer. Dozens from the Academy have tried to escape with their lives and only twenty have made it. To make it worse, I don't recall having seen many prisoners in the station. That tells me that they don't take many of them alive by any means. Although, what was I expecting? These are bounty hunters, or Rippers is what Roy called them, they are trained to hunt people down. It makes sense that not many people escaped with their lives. In fact, that makes them some of the luckiest people alive.

"So, why did y'all run away?" Roy asked as we went further into the tree line still following the tracks.

It took me a second to look back and take in what had happened. Everything occurred so quickly that I hardly had time to realize what I had just gone through.

"Robins set me up. He was planning on blowing up the pipeline, not caring who was there. Since his plan failed, he made sure that no one would say anything about it. Probably sentencing a kid to die, he killed the officers that took us in knowing I would say something about it. Now he wants me dead. My friends helped me escape," I explained looking at Linda who gave a sad smile.

"Ah, Robins. I remember him, everybody says he's the one tellin' the Rippers to kill people for no good reason," Roy said angrily. "What 'bout you, young lady?" turning to Linda.

"I ran after David. After I heard the bounty being announced on communications, I couldn't believe what I was hearing. I ran to our group to find out what happened to make sure David was fine. Connor had told me I just missed him. So I ran and I saw David running out of the building," Linda explained looking at me.

A moment of what seemed like slow motion occurred when we looked into each other's eyes. Her eyes sparkled and twinkled like the stars in the night sky. Just looking at her takes my breath away. Absolutely nothing compared to the beauty I was gazing upon at this very moment.

The silence was broken by Roy's angered grunt, "That scumbag pisses me off. He knows that no one would believe ya. That's why he never gets caught, cause everyone will side with the council," he vented. "He's crazy, ya know? No one knows why he wants to blow the Academy to smithereens. Power? Bloodthirsty? Who knows? Maybe both."

"I'll let you both in on a little secret. Our people are plannin' something against Robins. Without him, the Academy's corruption would end. We could live freely. But, I don't know everythin'. Y'all have to get there to the camp, the more the better," Roy explained.

Listening to Roy made me wonder what part of the Academy he must have been in.

After he was done talking I asked, "So, what were you a part of? What happened to you if I may ask?" I didn't want to strike a nerve if the past was too harsh.

Roy seemed to slow down his pace as the question came up. A frown took over Roy's face and began to talk.

"I was one of them. The Rippers, I mean. I was assigned a mission to hunt down a man who was labeled as a drug dealer and abuser. I got ta his house one night gettin' ready to take 'em in. I had gotten to his lawn when two Sweepers drove up ta me. They asked me to come with 'em. I asked why and they never told. I told them I wouldn't leave without an explanation, so they chose to bring out their blades and started to attack," Roy explained.

"I put up a hell of a fight, I didn't lose of course. But I did get this nasty scar," he said, pulling down the top of his coat and shirt, which revealed a large red scar going from the base of the neck and down into the collarbone.

My eyes widen at the once large gash in Roy's body. No words could come out of my mouth that could respond to his story or his severe scar. I could never know what that event must have been like or felt like. Although, now it might come true since I'm on the run from these Rippers. Which also means that the same thing could happen or I might even get killed. Now my hands are shaking and sweating just thinking about it.

The tracks began to turn to the left and continued so far

I couldn't see an end. Roy then came to a stop and turned towards us.

"This is as far as I'll go. Y'all must head straight towards the mountains," he says as he directs with his hand forward. "Y'all will need to hurry, them Sweepers will catch up quick. Be safe and be cautious, this will be your worst part of the journey."

"Thank you for everything, Roy. How could we ever repay you?" Linda asked.

"Y'all can get to the camp. That's how you'll repay me," Roy responded with a smile.

As he turned away, I twisted my head towards our destination. The trees covered most of the land and scaled the base of the mountains. They started dissipating further towards the top until there was no more, and only the snowy tops towered the region while being misted by the clouds. Looking up at this sight made me realize how long and difficult of a trip this was going to be. I cursed under my breath.

# 10

## DAVID

The trek had begun. So far the trip consists of the sound of our shoes crushing the leaves beneath us. Roy leaving us to walk towards the mountains renders me frightened, uncomforting and even paranoid. I constantly look around the trees hoping that a Ripper wouldn't be there. So far that is true, but maybe not for too long.

The woods seem still and quiet, not even the song of birds was heard. The day was bright with the sun gleaming through the treetops. A nice warmth filled the air along with a scent of wood and grass. Again, everything seems silent, a little too silent.

Linda and I walk in silence for almost half an hour. I decided to break the silence by asking, "So . . . you really didn't believe them when they called my bounty?"

"Well of course, why should I believe that? You're not the kind of person that would want to blow up a building, right?" she asked in a joking manner.

I chuckled, "I guess not. I just didn't think that someone would go out of their way to run after me."

"Of course I would do that. You're important to us," Linda reassured. "You're important to me."

That last sentence caught me off guard. I turn my head to her swiftly with eyes wide and face turning bright red. Linda smiled but continued to look forward. I'm thinking to myself, *Is this really happening? Did she really say that?* I had never been able to have the guts to talk to her about my emotions towards her. What she said just implied that she might like me. My stomach felt the fluttering sensation of butterflies once again. I was speechless, no words were able to come out.

Embarrassingly, all I could muster was, "I . . . uh . . . um."

She continued, "You know that you have very good friends who care about you. Connor never believed you did that and hates the Academy for accusing you. You're not alone."

Listening to that calms my nerves. The past several hours have been a period of paranoia. A series of waiting for the police to take me into trial and proceeding to run away from the Rippers that want to chop my head off. However, hearing

Linda's voice and listening to what she had to say made me feel serene.

Then my mind started to think about the note and where Mike and Roger got it and how. "Hey . . . so . . . how did Mike and Roger know where to go or how did they know about Roy?" I asked.

Linda squinted her face a little trying to think about it, "I'm not too sure. Mike just said that they were given a piece of paper as a kid and he told me to go to the shop that Roy had, but I followed you so it helped me."

I was puzzled and wondered how the two soullinked friends got to know about Roy and his shop. Although at this rate, I'll never be able to know. The mountains are the only place that I have to worry about getting to. Looking up towards the snow packed towers of earth just seemed impossible to get to. I sigh at the fact that this was gonna be a long journey.

Suddenly, I heard a noise coming from behind, the sound of a motor. Leaves and dirt flew upward as I looked behind. I stop walking, grab Linda's arm and turn to her and see a large bush in the distance and say, "Hide! Now!" pointing towards the bush.

We sprint for the hiding spot, sliding down a hill part of the forest scooping up dirt and leaves along the way down. The sound of the car seemed to rumble the earth below me as it got closer and closer.

I push with my legs to slip into the pile of leaves, vines and twigs. Linda falls in suit and we lay in the uncomfortable series of plants on our stomachs and stop moving. My levels of stress went from zero to a hundred in seconds, my heart beats in my throat once again. I feel my blood pumping rapidly throughout my head.

It was the Sweepers, the cars for the Rippers. The automobile slowed down and came to a stop right in eyesight, to where we were just standing. The black and menacing car stood for a second until the driver and passenger doors opened. The driver is a tall and burly looking man with a clean shaven face and short, red hair. The passenger is a shorter man with sideburns and a trenchcoat.

They didn't seem to notice us in the thick bush in the dense forest. In my head I'm telling myself that I hope they didn't see us over and over again. I trust my gut and stay absolutely still.

The burly man kneels down to the floor checking out the crushed leaves and scuffed ground. The one in the trench coat looked around thoroughly for any kind of movement.

The burly man cursed, "I can't get a good read, the tracks are screwed from the drive."

"I told you we should've stopped earlier," the passenger scolded.

"Shut up! It's not that hard to find Runaways like them. I know they didn't go far."

"That's what you said back in town. Now look where we are."

"Don't test me right now! Don't try it!" the burly man said, pointing a finger at his partner. "Just get back into the car and shut up, you hear me?"

His partner reluctantly sat back into the Sweeper, giving a big sigh of anger and annoyance.

"I think we're in the clear," I said while they started the car back up. I turn to Linda to reassure that we are alright.

Linda quickly pushed me down and yelled, "Duck!" as the Sweeper raced towards us. I planted my face against the ground just before the wheels of the car brushed over the bush we hid in. The rubber tore through the leaves and skidded right above my head, almost crushing me. Before I knew it, the Sweeper was gone and heading in the direction we've been walking towards. The sound of the roaring motor grew softer and softer until it was out of eyesight.

Linda and I get up out of the bush, brushing off some of the dirt. She turned to me and said, "Now we have to be even more careful. Cause now, they're going to be ahead of us this whole time."

The statement sent shivers down my spine. She was right of course. The Rippers were going to be in front of us the whole time.

# 11

**DAVID**

**E**very step I take seems to be the loudest one in the world. I hold my breath at times to keep the Rippers from hearing me if they were ever nearby. I couldn't stop looking over my shoulder and all around the silent and dense forest. The further I walk, the more paranoid I seem to get.

The sound of running water gradually became louder as we came across a creek that flowed from right to left. The setting sunlight glistened the crystal-clear water, revealing the sedimentary rocks that are slowly being washed away. Leading up towards the right is a small forest cave that seemed to only go about fifteen to twenty feet into the hill.

Linda walked in front of me, kneeling down towards the water and splashing it on her face. "We need to get to the next town soon. We don't have any provisions," Linda suggested.

"But what about the Rippers ahead of us?" I asked too worried to go anywhere that sounded exposed.

"We won't make it to the mountains without food and water. So yes, we have to risk it if we want to make it there."

I stood in silence, shuffling my feet in the ground as I knew that she was right. We don't even have a water bottle in our possession. "Well then, where would the next town be?" I asked.

Linda stood up, "If we keep going tomorrow, then we should be able to run into it. It should be Lone Camp that we run into if I remember the map correctly."

The sunlight was almost lost as the sky began to turn dark and slightly purple. I looked over at the small cave, "I guess that means camping for the night, probably in that cave," I suggested.

Linda looked over her shoulder and started nodding, "That'll be the plan, won't it?"

I began to gather twigs and sticks on the ground, "I'll start making a fire."

But Linda intervened, "No, we can't build a fire out here. It's too dangerous, we'd get caught by the Rippers now that they're in front of us."

I knew she was right, but the nights get cold and freezing

would be inevitable. I knew that I was afraid about the Rippers chasing us, however we need to stay warm if we want to live and that's what I intend to do. I drop my sticks that I was holding, "Alright, so what are we going to use for warmth? Winter is starting and we hardly have enough clothes to keep us warm."

She swiftly took my hand and started pulling me towards the cave. "We'll keep each other warm. Just sleep right next to me and we'll be fine," she said.

My mood shifted from frustration to bliss and surprise. Yes it was smart to give each other warmth in order to prevent us from being seen. Although, I didn't know she would suggest that so quickly. My face blushed and I answered with, "Oh . . . uh . . . okay," since I had nothing else in mind to answer with.

Walking inside the small cave is like walking into a glacier. The air around suddenly becomes colder. The ground is filled with dirt and gravel and the walls and ceiling made a perfect, spherical shape all around. There is nothing much to see as it becomes darker, just an empty and rocky perimeter.

Linda started kicking at some of the gravel on the ground, making a space for us both to sleep. "Ready when you are," she said, beginning to lie down.

I hesitate to lie down next to the person that I have had a crush on for months. In my head I'm thinking that I cannot mess this up. I want her to like me but I don't want to make her feel uncomfortable. Ironically though, I'm the one that is feeling awkward.

I walk on the other side of her and lie down on my side, pushing my back up against hers. Surprisingly enough, the ground here is not very uncomfortable. I'm able to give myself a position that will allow me to doze off. Now that I'm in such a position, my body begins to relax and my eyes become heavy.

"Goodnight, David," Linda said softly.

I'm too tired to respond and my eyes close.

My eyes open to see the rusty, iron bars of the jail cell. The walls around move in a snake-like motion with stains of red splattered in various places. I feel something dripping off my hands and looking down there is blood covering them like I had dipped them in red paint.

Turning back to the bars I could see the officer that brought me in groaning the words, "Help me!" The bars open and the man staggers his way towards me like a zombie. I'm paralyzed with fear, just standing there as the dying officer fell on top of me and bringing me down to the ground.

As I feel the impact of my body being slammed onto the ground, I cannot see the officer. Looking up I see the clouds. I stand up and look at my surroundings and see the Academy directly in front of me. To the right is Vance who is on the ground scrambling, pleading for Robins to stop. Robins is standing over him with bloody and bruised fists.

Robins kneels down to Vance and throws massive punches in his face, causing blood to fly and making his body go limp.

I couldn't believe what I just saw, my heart stopped in place. I couldn't breathe or talk.

Robins, standing over the body of Vance then turns to me and starts for a dead sprint. I turn around and start running as fast as I can. But the speed and strength of Robins took me down. Then a repeating and searing pain shot through my back. I realized that he was stabbing me over and over again with his blades. I try moving and fighting back, but I can't because of the pain.

He stopped suddenly and the sound of an explosion came from the Academy. Debris and fire fly everywhere, the heat is almost unbearable. I turn on my side looking up at my attacker who held his blades down to his side, doused in my own blood.

"You will never escape," he said menacingly. He then took his blade up and went for a final stroke.

I woke up with a jump and a yelp, sweating profusely. My breathing is heavy and I stopped in place sitting up.

"David? Are you alright?!" Linda asked, in a deeply worried tone.

I couldn't respond, my body is trying too hard to catch my breath. I then felt Linda's hands on my arm saying, "It's alright, it was just a nightmare. You're safe," she said, desperately trying to calm me down.

I begin to calm down after I realize that I was back in the cold and eerie cave. My panting stops after about a minute of Linda holding my hands and stroking them with her thumbs.

She then broke the silence and asked, "Do you want to talk about it?"

The dream replayed in my head and all I thought about was Robins and how much of a brutal killer he was. I couldn't get it out of my head, but I didn't want to cause any more concern with Linda.

"I think we just need to keep moving. Robins will catch us if we stay in one spot for too long," I finally responded.

"Robins doesn't know that we're here. We'll be safe for the rest of the night and we can keep moving in the morning," she said reassuringly.

"I think I'll just stay up for the rest of the night," I suggested. I'm wide awake now, there is no way I am going to sleep with an image like that in my head.

"David, you're going to need rest. I don't think that's a good idea."

"I'll be fine, plus we'll probably need a lookout anyway."

Linda looks at me with more worry than ever. I turn towards the entrance of the cave and lie down on my side, not changing my mind whatsoever. After a few seconds of hesitation, Linda lied down right beside me and started to drift off.

# 12

## ROBINS

**T**he day is over and the night has come, which means I was able to get away from the dysfunctional Academy for the night. I begin walking through town, feeling the cold air sweep through the streets. Most stores have already closed for the night, although I am on my way to the A&P store. Specifically for the pharmacy.

The town is silent, hardly any cars came rolling through town. One by one I see lights going out in most buildings such as apartments. Street lights are the only things lighting up the town now.

I come out of an alleyway and turn the left corner to the A&P store that seems to be the only one lit up in the whole block. Opposite to the store is a group of what look to be young adults smoking cigarettes and drinking alcohol. The smell of tobacco coursed through the air, pounding my nose.

I walk across the street towards the entrance of the store and into the building. Inside revealed a long line of registers, cabinets and desks all along the sides. Some registers are empty and only a few customers are buying something. The store sold a variety of products such as food, some accessories and medicines. I head towards the back to the right desk where a skinny man in a white button down shirt and black tie stood waiting for his last few customers. His hair was oily with gel that was held facing the side of his head.

As I get to the desk he makes a face that shows he's not surprised to see me, "Hey, Steven. How can I help you?" he said.

"Hey, Jeffrey. I need the usual," I responded.

"Really? Steven, I really should advise you to go see a doctor. Go to the hospital and see if you can treat this illness."

"They won't be able to do anything, I've said this multiple times. I need the Valium," I said, trying to keep calm. Valium was Diazepam, a drug that's supposed to treat anxiety and helps me with my temper. I've used it ever since this anger became a problem. I ran out a couple days ago, which caused the anger to worsen most likely.

Jeffrey sighs and goes under the desk to grab a small container with the label *Valium* on it. "That'll be thirteen dollars," he said.

Usually the tablets were around eleven dollars, but I didn't really care. All I know is that I need them. "They were less last time," I said, handing him the bills.

"Yeah well, I'm trying to get you to search for help without these drugs. We're running low so the prices are going up," he said, taking the money.

"I have all the help that I need," and I took the tablets.

"Take good care, Steven," Jeffrey said.

I nodded my thanks and began walking out the door with some stares from the other cashiers. Going outside I could see that the group of smokers and drinkers have moved to the alleyway that I usually go down. They laugh hysterically, most of them guys but one of them had a laugh of a fifteen year old girl.

I ignore them and begin to walk straight ahead, a different route back to the Academy. Once I cross the street another sound grabs my attention coming from the smoker gang. I look over to my left and there is a girl there that looks like she's just passing by. She was gorgeous, she had long red hair and pale skin. She was holding her arms like she was hugging herself tight indicating that she was uncomfortable. The guys there prevented her from moving any further and started to surround her.

They seem like they're trying to make her take something, some kind of drug. She shook her head no, but the boys kept harassing and pushing her around.

I walk towards them preparing to do something about these idiots. I yelled at them, "Hey, leave her alone!"

They all turned to me and paid no attention to the helpless girl who is now getting out of their grasp and running away. They wore leather jackets and combed back, greasy hair.

They started laughing, "Or what, grandpa? What're you going to do, huh?" the one in the middle said. There are five of them and now they begin to surround me like the girl.

"Trust me, you don't want to know," I warned them.

The leader smiled and then looked down at the tablets I am holding in my hand. But before I could put them in my pocket, one of his minions to my left quickly snatched it out of my grasp.

The boy who took it, looked at it and said, "Man, you've been taking the wrong stuff."

"Yeah, you should try something a little more fun," the leader added and pulled out a small tube from his pocket. He opens it and takes out a small tablet and I realized that it is acid or LSD.

"Here, old man. Take this, it's better," he said, walking closer to me.

"Don't bother, I'm good with what I've got," I refused.

The leader frowned and became frustrated, "Take it now."

Then his friend directly behind me pushed me towards him. My anger began to build up once again. "Don't do this, boy. Or you'll regret it," I warned once again.

But that didn't work, he just laughed and said, "Take it, grandpa or I'll make you."

My head heats up, my breathing becomes heavy and my fists clench up. His friends shove me even harder, almost knocking me to the ground.

At that moment, my rage unleashes and my face turns red and I scream in anger. I take the leader, lift him off the ground and slam him back down with all my strength. His friends flinched and looked at one another. I go for the next one to my right and throw a left hook which swings home to the side of his head, knocking him straight to the pavement. One goes in behind and puts me in a chokehold and pulls me backwards.

But he wasn't ready for what I had to offer. I take his arms and throw him over my shoulder, making him land straight on his back. I kneel down to him and start beating him with my fist, causing bruises to form and blood spatter. The last two guys try shoving me off and send a series of punches to my face. I turn to my right and tackle the guy punching me and drive him straight into the wall of a building. The impact caused something to pop and the boy screamed in pain.

The last one begins kicking me in the legs and stomach, sending waves of pain from the stomach down. As soon as he throws one more kick, I grab it and sweep his leg. Once he is on the ground, I kneel down once again and throw punch after punch after punch into his face until he is knocked out.

Every single one of the guys there is either unconscious or groaning in pain. I see the leader trying to stand up, so I run over and kick him down, knocking the wind out of him. I turn away, pick up my pills and walk away, leaving them in their own pools of blood.

# 13

## ROBINS

oing around the next alley to the right, I continue to hit trash cans and brick walls that scratch up my knuckles good. My head is pounding and throbbing in pain as I continue to unleash my rage onto inanimate objects.

All of a sudden, I hear a voice behind me say, "Councilman Robins?" in a whimpering tone. I turn around to see Vance standing there with the blade I gave to him out and dripping with blood. His face is pale and his arms and legs are shaking.

My rage dialed down and I became calm enough to walk over to the quivering boy. Not caring about the piercing pain in my head I said, "Vance? Aren't you supposed to be in Europe or something by now?"

"I tried to get out . . . but . . . the Hunters . . . there were too many," he responded. He begins to sniffle and tears run down his face. "I had to do it," he said and I realized that the blood came from a Hunter.

"He was going to kill me. I tried to hide, but they chased me," he explained.

I don't know what to say, the boy is stunned and panicked. I thought that he already made it out of the city. However, it doesn't matter now. I have to assist him in some way. I didn't save him just for him to get caught again. This boy is meant to live and that's what I'm going to help him do.

I kneel down to him and say, "You'll be fine. I will help you escape, I'll help you get out of here."

He looked at me with a sparkle in his teary eyes. "Really?" he said sniffling.

I nodded, "You're safe with me. But first, we need to change your appearance. You need new clothes and hair color."

Vance touched his hair with his non-blade hand, "Hair color?" he asked.

I nodded again, "We'll get some dye from one of the stores."

I stand up and start walking into town with Vance just under my wing. We walk out of the alleyway and back onto the street of the A&P store and the smoking gang members who are still lying there on the street and sidewalk. I show Vance the opposite direction of them towards a wide variety of stores such as clothing shops, gas stations, barber shops and more.

I look around in the dark and starry night until I see the Weiland and Harrison Clothing shop. All the lights are off and the doors are locked. I look in my jacket pocket and pull out a lock-picking tool. Hunters have these in order to get into places where a bounty could be staying or hiding in a public place.

After a few seconds of maneuvering in the lock, I'm able to open the door. I put the tool back in my pocket and gestured to Vance to come inside with me quietly. We walk in and take a look at the sections of clothes that hang everywhere around the room. I grab a couple of coats, a blue and green winter coat and compare them to Vance's size. I switched back and forth to see which is better. The green one seemed a better fit, so I hung up the blue one back onto the hanger.

I grab a green collar shirt, slim pants and loafer shoes that suit him nicely. I hand the clothes to Vance and we silently sneak out and close the door without being spotted by anyone.

I scanned the area to see if anyone saw us and luckily no one was there. I take Vance further down the street towards an intersection. At the corner is a Salon called Mini's. I once again use the pick locking tool to get inside the Salon. Inside there are seats on the sides and back, the sides facing mirrors. Each one has a small drawer and I look in every one of them. One in the middle held a bottle of brown hair dye.

The dye was all he needed in this salon, so I closed the drawer and walked out with Vance. The last thing that Vance needs is a place to spend the night. I couldn't bring him back to the Academy, way too risky. I must find the nearest motel. We walk down the street once again and turn left towards the outer edge of the town where a motel sits quietly with hardly any cars parked in the lot. I pick up the pace to a fast walk and Vance tries to keep up.

It is a fairly nice motel, not too ruggedy and pretty clean with two floors of rooms. The small building for the receptionist sat in the middle of this L shaped motel complex. We walk in and see a woman at the register that looks as if she is about to fall asleep.

Her head shot up like a rocket, smiled and said, "Good evening, how can I help you?"

"We just need a room for the night," I responded quickly.

"Alright, that'll be thirteen dollars and eighty-five cents."

I pull out a roll of dollar bills and give her a twenty dollar bill. "Keep the change," I said.

Her eyes widened a bit and quickly pulled out a key, "Your room is 205. Enjoy your stay."

Rapidly I take the key and walk out towards the rooms. We take the stairs leading to the second floor and towards room 205 which is fairly close to the stairs. I unlock the door using the room key and walk right in and immediately close the door behind me as Vance swiftly moves in.

I sigh in relief and take in the scenery of the room. The fresh and new room smell filled the air. A couple of nicely made, white beds sit to the left and a television directly in front of them. The walls are covered in red and white stripes. The bathroom is towards the back and the brown curtains cover the window right next to the entrance door.

Vance lies the clothes down and sits on the bed next to them, still looking like he saw the devil.

"We'll leave in the morning, most likely for a train," I said.

Vance looked at me uncomfortably and said, "Why are you still helping me? Earlier it looked like you were going to . . . you know . . ." he couldn't get any further.

This time I felt guilty. This kid should be confused after what I said to him and almost coming after him in a blind rage. I felt terrible for him. "I didn't mean to get angry or to cause you any harm. You shouldn't have to pay for the mistakes I made. I just can't control it most of the time, kid. I'm so sorry," I apologized profusely.

Vance looked at me with sympathy, not knowing what to say or do.

"I don't want to hurt people, kid," I reassured. "Let's just get some sleep. You have a big day tomorrow."

I lay on the other bed, take off my shoes and wait until my eyes get droopy and fall asleep.

14

# ROBINS

wake up expecting to see my room that I'm used to at the Academy. Yesterday felt like a dream, like it didn't happen. Although, I realize that I'm at the motel with Vance sleeping soundly on the bed nearest to the bathroom. I sit up in my bed and look over at the boy in the other bed.

All I can think about when I see Vance is Laura and how she was around kids. She loved being around them and always made them happy. Her kindness was intoxicating and contagious.

I wish I could be more like her, although it wasn't my field of expertise unfortunately. My main goal is to get Vance to safety and that's what I would be most proficient with. I rise up out of my bed, walk over to Vance, and lightly shake him awake. "We have to get ready, kid," I said softly.

Vance groaned, eventually woke up with squinted eyes, and moved in a sluggish fashion. He sits up, slowly taking off the sheets and shifting his legs over the side of the bed. I take him to the bathroom where I will dye his hair.

Bringing the bottle of dye with me, I have Vance stand over the sink as I open the bottle and spread some dye on my hands. I then rubbed the contents into his dirty blond hair and scrubbed it around his head. I noticed the blistered burn marks all around the boy's neck, causing me to slow down the scrubbing. I look away from them, grab a little more dye from the bottle, and scrub some more in order to make a more apparent color of brown.

After several minutes of scrubbing the dye around, I bent his head down into the sink and washed the residue off. I grab a white towel to dry off his hair that eventually turns brown as well.

"Alright, go change into your new outfit, kid," I told him.

Vance obeys without saying a word and takes his stolen clothes into the bathroom. It didn't take him very long to change, a couple minutes max was all he needed. He came out with his collar button down shirt, slim pants and his new loafer shoes that fit him quite nicely. I hand him the coat that he puts on immediately and before I know it, he looks like a totally different person.

"Perfect. Now, let's go catch you a train," I said, heading for the door.

Heading outside is like entering a freezer. The cold ripped the breath from my chest as I bundled myself up in my own jacket. The morning sun hasn't quite lit up the sky yet, although the color is turning a sunrise orange. I close the door behind me and we head downstairs and north towards the train station.

Walking up the streets and turning several corners, we see the building that is the train station. It is more of a pavilion that covers the seating areas and the ticket station in front. The station is near the forest and part of the outer edge of the town. We see fewer and fewer buildings as we walk closer to the station. Most people seemed to be wanting to catch the early trains at the moment as we watched several people walk up to buy a ticket.

The man who is selling the tickets yells, "Next," after selling to a couple walking in with interlocking arms.

I walk up to the window that separates us and say, "I need a ticket for the next train."

"Are you looking to go anywhere in particular, sir? Or are you just wanting the next one to Dallas, Texas?" he asked for confirmation.

"Dallas is fine."

"Alright, that'll be four dollars, sir," he said, pulling out one ticket.

I reached into my jacket pocket and pulled out four dollar bills when he asked, "Do you need a second one, sir?" while looking at Vance.

"Oh no, just the one is fine. He'll be seeing his grandparents once he gets there," I lied.

The man passed me the ticket and took the money I put on the counter and said, "Have a nice day." I nodded my thanks and gestured to Vance to follow me towards the train.

We follow the crowd of people under the pavilion to wait for the next train when I notice something apprehensive. Out of the corner of my left eye I see droplets of blood coming from a closet door. I look around to see if anyone noticed and so far everyone has managed to walk past it. They are tiny droplets, something people might not notice right away or wouldn't think much of it.

"Vance, stay close," I tell him as I walk towards the door.

Opening it I see cleaning supplies such as brooms and mops with shelves lined with chemicals. On the floor is the body of a man lying in a pool of his own blood. The man looked familiar with his white mustache and bald head.

"Who is that?" Vance asked behind me in a perturbed tone.

I sighed with guilt and anger, "He was an old friend, my therapist in fact. I haven't talked to him in years." I look at his injuries and notice the two parallel entry wounds in his stomach. The sign that a Hunter had killed him.

"You want to know why I want the Academy gone, kid?" I began. "It's because of things like this that infuriate me. The Hunters are killing good people and I don't understand why. I'm not the one initiating some of these bounties and whoever is loves the killing spree."

At that moment, I felt a sharp object on my left shoulder

coming from something or someone in the room. "Don't move and I won't kill either of you," a voice said.

# 15

## DAVID

I watch the sunlight progressively getting brighter throughout the forest. I couldn't fall back asleep, not even close. Just lay there waiting for the night to end while hearing the sounds of crickets, frogs and numerous birds. The cold air slowly became warmer with the sunlight.

As the morning came, I could feel Linda shifting awake. She inhaled deeply and sat up with a yawn. I began to sit up as well, anxious to get moving. Linda looked at me with tired eyes and said, "Good morning."

I gave her a smile, "Morning."

"Did you get any sleep at all?" she asked, implying the nightmare I had last night.

I shook my head, "I'm fine, I wasn't very tired anyway," I lied. In fact, I'm exhausted from the series of unfortunate events that took place yesterday.

Linda gave another worried look, "Are you sure you're alright?"

"I said I'm fine. I just want to get to the next town and get to those mountains," I responded, a bit irritated.

We stand up and continue our journey through the forest. We hop along the rocks of the creek to get across the running water and continue through the trees and brush. Neither one of us talked while hiking towards Lone Camp. I'm too exhausted and irritated to come up with anything to start a conversation. The trek started off in silence, not even the sounds of birds chirping are heard throughout the canopy of the trees.

Linda was the first to speak, "If you ever want to talk about it, I'm here for you. It seemed like a pretty bad nightmare," she insisted.

I didn't want to say anything rude coming from the irritation. I sighed and said, "I don't really want to talk about it. But I appreciate you being here for me."

She didn't respond, however the silence was enjoyable so I was glad. After walking for about twenty minutes, the forest dissipated into a clearing that revealed the town of Lone Camp.

A small village consisting of rundown houses, a scarce supermarket and very few people.

We walked along the dirt road that led straight into town and entered the small grocery store in the center of the area. Not much is in here, small stacks of fruit, vegetables and meats are sitting in multiple baskets. Cans of beans and bags of snacks lie on shelves near the registers and the corners of the stores. Bottles of soda pops and juices sit in a refrigerated aisle along the side.

Linda grabs a basket and we begin looking for anything that would fill us up and keep us hydrated. Something doesn't feel right walking through this store and my eyes dart around nervously for anything peculiar. Linda grabs various jars and cans of goods for our journey, not cautiously looking for anything out of the ordinary like me.

Then, I see a few aisles down a couple of men that are looking straight at us. Both seem about the same height, both having brown hair and one is wearing eye glasses. Both are wearing winter coats, the one with glasses wearing a rusty zipper jacket and the other with a cowboy style coat.

They quickly walk around the aisles towards us and I grab Linda's arm. "We have to go now!" I say.

"What's wrong?" Linda asked puzzled.

I pointed towards the Rippers, "That's what's wrong! Now let's go!"

Linda drops the basket and we both dash out the door and once again head for the mountains. The Rippers ran as well but towards their Sweeper, which is parked to the side of the store. They briskly got in and turned the car on.

"Follow me! I know a place near here that we could use," Linda said, darting for the trees a little to the left of the mountains.

She runs in front of me and I follow her sliding down a hill full of dead leaves. My heart began to beat faster as I could hear the sound of the motor getting closer towards us with the rumble of the wheels getting more and more violent heading down the hill.

# 16

## DAVID

Sweat pours down my face, my legs burn and my heart is racing at a million miles an hour. The sound of the Sweeper quickly grows closer and closer as we sprint through the trees. We kick up dirt and leaves with each step that we take.

I take a quick glance backwards to see that the Sweeper has jumped the top of the hill and is now racing towards us down the slope. I speed up and continue to follow Linda, knowing that she was taking us to a place that could help us. I don't know what this place is, although I didn't care much at the moment as we are being chased by Rippers.

I looked back once again to see that the Sweeper is so significantly close. I grab Linda and throw ourselves to the left to prevent us from being run over. The front of the Sweeper scraped my shoes and pushed me forward as we dove into the leaves.

The car immediately slowed to a stop, knowing that they must've missed us. I help Linda up and we continue to run. The Sweeper reversed to turn towards us, slamming into a tree and almost breaking it. They accelerate once again to catch up to us.

There is another clearing that Linda leads us to, not as large as the one at Lone Camp. The clearing shows a complex, a few buildings that are connected by smaller entryways making a semi-circle facing our right. The one in the middle seemed to be a garage of some sort and the rest are plain, rectangular buildings made of red brick.

"Inside!" Linda screamed heading for the left building door. The car heads straight for us as we begin to open the door, not looking like they want to slow down. Linda swings it open and pulls me in with all her strength. As I got in, I could feel the gust of air from the car come upon us. The Sweeper bashed into the wall, decimating the door and the wall around it, causing me and Linda to fall backwards. They nearly got us, very nearly.

I'm stunned, overwhelmed and petrified. I thought I was dead, the whole thing seems unreal. My heart had stopped and all I did was sit there until Linda took my hand and said, "Get up! We have to go!" She pulled me up towards another door, not giving me time to look at the room. What was left of it anyways.

Through the door is a long hallway with doors lined up on each side symmetrically. There are the lone double doors towards the end of the corridor and nothing else. Just a straight shot towards another unknown room, at least to me.

"Come on! We're almost there!" Linda said.

"What are we supposed to do here?" I ask while on the run.

"We fight, and we're going to need weapons," she said, reaching the doors and swinging them open.

The room is significantly larger, looking much like a dojo. The walls are lined with Ripper blades, guards, helmets and face armor. The floor is painted over with lines making three large squares in the front, middle and back of the room going down a column towards us.

Linda had already reached for two different sets of blades and handed one to me. "Put this on and push the handle forward, hurry!" she said, putting on the other herself and strapping it in.

I followed her movements, much more panicked but still able to slip through the straps and tightened them. She showed how to activate the blades by grabbing the handle with her thumb and pushing forward. The blades came out with a sound like a sword coming out of a scabbard.

"How are we supposed to beat these guys when they've trained years for this?" I asked, doubting that we'll be able to stand up against them.

"Do you have a better idea? We can't outrun them nor hide from them now," Linda responded. "Just lead them to the other room towards the garage."

At that moment, the Rippers crashed through the double doors and revealed their own blades. The one in glasses said, "C'mon, just give up already. No use in running or fighting."

Neither one of us responds and instead prepares for a fight for our lives. The hunter in glasses then said, "Have it your way," and began to swing their blades.

The one in the cowboy style winter coat comes after me and swings horizontally. By shear instinct I open my blades and put them up to block the swing coming to the left side of my face. Adrenaline rushed through my veins and now the Ripper was swinging and jabbing all around.

I could hear the contact of metal on metal to my right where Linda is, sounding like she knows what to do with the blades. However, I need to focus on my fight and my life. The Ripper swings vertically now and I manage to jump to the left and dodge it. What I didn't realize was that he then swung back up and cut my right shoulder, sending a wave of pain throughout my arm.

I back away, stumbling and holding my bladed shoulder and heading for the door towards the garage. Linda is nearly blocking and dodging a series of stabs and swings of her own coming from the man in glasses. One vertical swing that she blocked knocked to her knees and made her stumble towards us at the door.

I shoved the doors open with all my force while the Ripper

pursuing me slices at my leg and creates a deep gash in my calf. I fell onto the ground, scrambling to get back up with all the pain that the man caused. I turn towards him and just barely block his jab towards my stomach with my own blades. He pushed with all his might and forced me backwards into the doors leading to the garage.

My back bashed against the doors and then into something metal. I pushed his blades to the left side of me, scraping the metal I had just been shoved into. I realized that this is a car, another Sweeper in fact. This is a garage for the Sweepers and a workshop indicated by the tools and gadgets sitting on benches and hanging on shelves.

The Ripper swung horizontally again with a right hook and back hand with his blade. I back out of the way, protecting my face with the blades. Suddenly he took an uppercut with his blades, slicing my right arm and my cheek. I'm sent to the ground, exhausted and overwhelmed. I slide myself backwards away from my assailant as Linda and the other Ripper burst through the doors.

The cowboy Ripper walked over me and went for a finishing stab to my chest. I quickly raised my blade to interlock it with his, making a cross with the daggers. The points are inches from my heart, which is beating rapidly. He continues to push down with all his weight upon my injured arm. I tried to support it with my left hand but that hardly seems to work. I knew this might be the end, I didn't have the strength. I didn't have the energy to fight back.

Suddenly the Ripper stumbles with the sound of a metal tool

smashing against his head. He rolls over to my side and standing above me is Linda with a large wrench. The Ripper stands back up and goes for another slash. I take the advantage and jab my blades straight into the man's chest, sending splatters of blood on his shirt and coat. He gasps in pain, not being able to say a word and slowly slid down on the wall and went limp.

I took out my blades from his body and laid down on my back gasping for air. The pain began to set in throughout my arm, leg and face. Sweat ran down my face into my wound which only made it sting. I groan in pain when I see Linda standing above me.

"David! Are you alright?" she asked in the most worried tone possible.

"I'm . . . fine," I mumbled.

"Let me get you some supplies to patch those up. I'll only be a minute."

"Wait," I said. Linda looked over at me and I continued, "How did you do all that?"

She looked confused, "All what?"

"The fighting and the blades, how did you do that?" I repeated.

"I was supposed to be one of them, but then I quit."

"Oh," I said, almost delirious.

Linda shook her head, "Let me get you those supplies."

"So I guess we'll stay here for a bit, huh?" I asked as she got up.

"Seems like it," she responded.

# 17

## DAVID

After lying on the ground with blood leaking from my arm, leg and face, Linda comes back with a bag of medical supplies and a crutch. She sets the bag down next to me and kneels down to tend to my wounds. My injuries stung and burned so much I couldn't move my body without it hurting more.

Linda starts on my left calf and takes out a brown bottle and says, "This will sting a little." She opened it and poured the contents on the gash.

My body jerks away and immediately a sensation of a thousand red hot needles seizes my calf. I scream in pain, still not able to sit myself up. Linda covers the wound in white cloth and wraps the injury in gauze and medical tape.

My fists clench and my body tenses after the first round of pain. Now Linda moves to my shoulder, taking off the jacket and the shirt. She poured more of the liquid, which I now realize is hydrogen peroxide, and began to wrap it as well. The piercing pain went from my leg to my shoulder now after the next wound was cleaned, making me grit my teeth as she wrapped the gauze around.

Now she was moving to the right side of my face. I cursed as I knew what was to come next. I look into her beautiful blue eyes that remind me of the ocean. I wish I could stare into them longer, but she was already moving my head to the right to allow the hydrogen peroxide to pour down my face without getting in my eyes.

She gave no hesitation and poured the liquid onto my cheek, making my face squint in agony. This time she grabbed butterfly bandages and stuck them horizontally on my face, perpendicular to the scratches that the Ripper made.

Finally, the procedure was done. I am relieved, but still hurting. Linda helps me to sit up slowly and asks, "How do you feel?"

I sighed, "Better," I said. "So, you were supposed to train as a Ripper?"

She frowned, "I didn't want to. It was something that I entered to please my parents. They took us to this place, the

Academy Training Camp, for beginners. I learned a thing or two here but I told the council I wanted to switch to communications as I thought I would be more useful there. I hadn't told my parents about that because I knew they would refuse. So the council moved me and they had no choice but to let me. That was about five years ago."

"Wow, it's probably good you did that, otherwise you wouldn't have met us," I said, giving a smile.

Linda smiled back and chuckled, "Yeah, and I'm glad I did."

She made me feel like my injuries didn't exist for a moment. That moment was over once she said, "Alright, let's get you on this crutch."

She pulls my left arm and I strain to get back up with a grunt of pain. I use the workbench with my injured arm to help myself up, making it more painful. Eventually, I'm able to get back on my feet, or foot for that matter. I didn't put any pressure on my left leg since the wound is too painful. Linda put the crutch under my left armpit which gave me leverage, giving my left leg support while I put minimal pressure on it.

"Alright, I guess we should start heading for the camp now," I suggested.

"Woah, slow down. You should get used to the crutch first before we continue," Linda counter suggested.

"What about the Rippers? We can't stay here for very long. They'll be looking for the ones we just . . . you know."

"I know, but you're in no condition to travel right now. You need some strength back. It's still a long trip," Linda reasoned.

I knew she was correct, although on the inside I wanted

to continue. I didn't want to waste any time to get to our safe haven. However, it seems like the trip is going to have to be delayed for some time.

I looked down at myself, remembering that I don't have a shirt on. "Um . . . maybe we should get some new clothes," I said awkwardly.

Linda laughed, "C'mon, I know a room," and she walked towards the next door past the Sweepers.

I admired the cars as I limped towards her and said, "Can't we just take one of these to the mountains?"

Linda shook her head, "There's no use, the Sweepers come with a special code that you have to enter in. Only the driver knows the code, and these ones at the camp change every month," she explained.

She holds the door open for me, leading into the next small grey hallway. The crutch became easier to use every step I took with it. I limp to the next door that Linda kindly opens for me once again and opens into another large room.

This room contained all sorts of drawers, cabinets and lockers. Some cabinets are already open in the far left corner, indicating the place where Linda got all the medical supplies. The middle of the room contains chairs facing towards our left to a chalkboard with no writing on it.

Linda walks over to the lockers on our right behind the sets of chairs and opens multiple. She pulls out a camouflaged jacket that perfectly matches the trees and bushes outside.

"This will make it hard for Rippers to see us while we walk

out there. If not impossible," Linda presented in a model-like fashion.

I smiled, "Please, do tell more."

She reaches into the locker again and pulls out a backpack, "This has all our food, equipment for travel and," she gasps in a joking manner, "a water canteen," she says in a musical tone.

She is so cute, I thought. She managed to lift my spirits even after a near death experience. I don't know what I would do without her. She knows what to do, where to go and her presence is just heartwarming.

She walks over to me with a shirt and a jacket. She had me lift my arms and slip the sleeves through my hands and over my head. I wince in pain as I lift my right shoulder. She then swung the jacket around and put my arms through the sleeves.

After putting on the jacket, everything appeared to slow down once again. Those ocean blue eyes looked directly into mine and made me stand still. I could stay like this for a while, I thought. She was amazing, like something out of a fantasy book. Like a princess I thought. I want to say something so badly, or do something about this moment. *Maybe a kiss?* I didn't know. I've never been in a situation like this before.

I don't want to mess anything up, I thought. So I broke the silence and said, "W . . . we should probably get going now, I'm feeling better now with the crutch."

"Oh, right. I'll . . . get the door," she said, looking a little disappointed.

That's when I realized I probably should've done something.

Ironic that I didn't want to mess up anything and now I think I just did. Now she is opening the door leading outside. I limp onto the dirt and look in the direction of the mountains.

Hovering over and through the mountains are dark clouds, possibly storm clouds blowing towards us. Although it appeared far enough away for us to continue and be able to find shelter along the way. However, that is just going off of hope and guesses. Hopefully, if those are storm clouds, it'll blow over by the time we start climbing the mountain.

"Stand up and turn to me slowly," the Hunter said.

I am becoming furious, the thought of a good friend dying to one of my own men made my blood boil. Someone is initiating these bounties that aren't me and that makes me even more angry. I have the desire to hurt this man, I want to destroy him so badly.

I stand up and turn to my left to face him and reveal who I am. The Hunter's oval shaped face turned from serious to fear.

He realized that I am his boss and immediately put the blades down. "I . . . I . . . sir . . . I didn't know," he quivered.

I take advantage and lunge at him, grabbing his throat and shoving him against the wall. "Who authorized a bounty on this man?" I said grinding my teeth in fury.

The Hunter choked and gargled because of my grasp, "I thought . . . it . . . was you . . . sir."

"I never placed a bounty on him! He was a good man!" I said.

"Please . . . don't," he begged.

My fists became white, winding up and ready to throw countless punches. But then, Vance stepped in, "Don't hurt him! He didn't know!"

I heard his voice, pleading to not hurt the man that had just murdered my friend. My fist shakes in rage, ready to be thrown at the man's face. But, like a miracle, I am able to put my fist down. Something stopped me from absolutely pummeling this man. Something about how Vance said those few words was able to dial down my anger.

I let go of his neck and back away, allowing a light headache to set in. The Hunter gasped for air, relieved that he didn't get destroyed. He holds his throat as if his insides are about to fall out.

"Are you alone?," I asked.

The Hunter looked up at me, "No. My partner is going on the train," he said.

I look outside of the room to see that the train has already stopped at the station, receiving all the people waiting. The sound of the whistle is heard all across town and the smoke at the top begins to spurt out.

"Who is the person you are hunting?" I demanded.

The Hunter quickly reaches into his pocket, grabs a photo and hands it to me. I yank it out of his hands and become shocked to see Jeffrey, the man selling and prescribing the Valium to me. It is a picture of him at his register in the A&P store.

I begin to run for the train, but it is already leaving. I sprint across the waiting area trying to catch the back end of the train. The back was able to get past the corner before I could catch it. It left me the one option of running, and I wasn't going to catch a train by running. I need a vehicle.

I turn to the Hunter and Vance who are running up to me. "Where is your Sweeper?" I ask desperately.

"It's in the front, sir," he answered obediently.

"Are you the driver?"

"Yes, sir."

"I need the code now! And the keys!" I said.

"Um, it's 3874, councilman," he responded quickly while handing me the keys.

"Let's go, Vance. We're getting you on that train!"

I waste no time in trying to reach the Sweeper, which is right where the Hunter had said. It is sitting in front of the train station, parked over to the right of it. I immediately unlock the door and jump into the driver's seat with Vance getting into the passenger's seat. The keypad sits to the left of the steering wheel and I punch in the numbers to start the Sweeper. I turn the keys and the car rumbles awake. I turn the Sweeper to the right, around the station and begin to follow the tracks that lead into the woods.

The car jumps around as we run over bumps, divots and logs. Dirt and dust fly up as the wheels grind on the earth. I follow the side of the tracks, avoiding the treeline.

"I need to find the other Hunter before he gets to another one of my friends. Once I'm able to do that you can stay on the train and you'll be able to get out of here and live a free life, got it?" I explained.

"Thank you, sir," Vance responded.

"You're going to get to safety. No matter what," I reassured.

Vance said nothing.

I resume the drive towards the train which we are catching up to. I floor the gas to ensure that we will be able to catch up. Some trees seemed to be leaning into the tracks and I managed to either break through them or move past the trunks. Hitting the branches did nothing to the car and only made the branches more flimsy or broke all together.

Finally we arrive at the back of the train which shows a rail and a back door. I ride next to it and press a button in the middle next to the radio to open the top ceiling window. "I know this is crazy, but you'll have to jump onto the back," I said to Vance.

He looked terrified, "I can't do that!" he said.

"Yes you can, trust me. You have to get on there if you're escaping to safety."

Vance then reluctantly gets up and starts getting on top of the car. I move ever so slightly closer to the rail. I hold it as steady as I can, waiting for Vance to take his leap. Suddenly, the Sweeper jumped from a bump in the ground, causing Vance to fly towards the rail. In a split second, Vance manages to hang on tight, get over the rail, and stay on his feet.

Now it was my turn. I didn't know exactly what I was going to do. I couldn't do what Vance did because there would be no gas. I thought for a second that I could give myself time to jump if I have enough distance.

I speed up the car to get further ahead of the back. I get the car about halfway up the train and I keep the car steady. Once I thought I was ready, I took my foot off the gas and opened my door. I ready myself to jump out of the car and onto the rail. The train speeds past me and before I know it, the rail reveals itself and I spring off the car.

I nearly fell off, managing to catch the rail with my hands at the last second. Vance helps me up by grabbing my shoulders and pulling me with all his might. I catch my footing and I heave myself up and over the rail. Now I was catching my breath, thinking that that could've been the end of me just now.

"Now . . . we have to find Jeffrey. Before the Hunter kills him," I said, beginning to open the door.

# 19

## ROBINS

tepping inside the train shows rows of seats facing each other with tables standing in between them. The seats are cushioned and comfortable for each passenger who is either looking out the window or giving strange looks at me and Vance.

A couple of young men play a game of cards while waiting for their stop who sit to the left. A couple of young ladies chat softly to one another as we pass by them to our right. A man and a woman sat next to each other on the left, passed the guys playing cards, who seemed to be talking about us as we shuffled by. To the left in the corner is a snoring old man with his fedora hat hanging over his face.

None of the seats have Jeffrey sitting in them, neither did we see the Hunter. I quickly go for the door to the next car. Rapidly I slide open the two doors entering the second to last car to reveal more people in the rows of seats. One man stands up, having his back turned to me, from the right side which is blocking my way of movement.

I shove him out of the way, making room for myself and Vance while he yelled, "Hey!" as he stumbles on the seat. I don't look back, only worrying about the man that is in trouble in one of the cars on this train. I search seat after seat hoping I would catch either the Hunter or Jeffrey, preferably Jeffrey first before he's taken out.

The seats in this car contain a family of four, mother, father and two children with both being girls. One man looked particularly creepy with a shaking hand holding a pocket watch that he seemed to like staring at. Then there is a couple making out in the corner which disturbed me and made Vance cringe.

I continue to move through the next car, at the same time making sure that Vance is still right behind me. Knowing that Vance was still next to me, I went back to rapidly checking each seat within the train. I'm beginning to wonder if the Hunter had already terminated him. That we must have missed him already and that we were too late. The stress builds up in my head and the worry synced into my chest like a large needle.

Not having any luck for these carts brings me guilt and the anxiety starts to take over until I see Jeffrey sitting on the left with his back turned to me on the fourth car. Sitting behind him, creeping around the seat is the Hunter. He has a pretty face but with a large nose and with luscious dark brown hair. He began to tuck his thumb under the handle to release the blade that is hidden under his sleeve.

I don't hesitate, and lunge for the Hunter's blade hand just before he could swing around to cut his bounty. I grab his arm with my right and wrap my left arm around his neck to tackle him to the ground. A lady yelps in the front part of the car and proceeds to run out of the car.

I put my full weight on him to prevent him from getting up, but he got his leverage, pushed up with his legs, and elbowed me in the stomach with his blade hand or his right for that matter. My body jerks back at the immense force that the Hunter fought with. He swung his blade in a horizontal motion, causing me to back away.

The Hunter then came back with his blade in another horizontal fashion, which gave me an opening to counter. As he comes around with his blades, I get in close and snatch his blade arm with both my hands and swing him around, throwing him into the right window of the train. The glass cracked severely as the Hunter staggered on the table.

I take the advantage, grab him by the top of his jacket, and slam him into the cracked window, shattering the glass. His head is now hanging outside of the train, causing the Hunter to frantically try to pull himself back in. However, I had him locked as I put my hand on the back of his neck and squeezed, refusing to let him back in.

Before I can do anything else, I feel tugs on my own jacket from behind and a voice saying, "Don't kill him! We need him!" I held the Hunter, thinking about what to do next. I grunt and pull him back into the train.

The Hunter, gasping for air, has large cuts and scrapes on his face. Mainly on his left cheek and forehead. He sits up on one of the seats and glances up at me. His face turned into horror and he said, "Councilman Robins, I . . . I'm so sorry! Please! Forgive me!"

I stare at him, still wondering who authorized this attack. "Who gave the order to hunt down Jeffrey?" I asked as calmly as I could.

The Hunter's face turned from horror to mystification, "I got the orders from communications, having notifications that it was from you, sir."

Someone is definitely giving false authorization to place a bounty on people. The bounties are supposed to be authorized by me since I am the councilman for hunting. However, someone is placing a bounty on good people, people that have done no wrong to the public. Not only that, but they are saying it was from me.

"Steven?" Jeffrey called from hiding behind one of the seats. "What's going on?"

"It's alright, Jeffrey. Just stay on the train, get to a far destination. You're better off staying there, you'll be safe," I assured.

I turn to the Hunter, who is still recovering on the seat, "Hunter, do you have a name?"

He stood up, "Kenneth, sir."

"Kenneth, you have a new task that is going to officially and personally be authorized by me and me only. Do you understand?"

"Understood, sir. What do you need me to do?" he asked.

"You're going to help me figure out who is placing these false bounties and make sure it doesn't happen again," I responded.

He nods in understanding and pulls out a map, "I suggest that we get off near the Training Camp. So that we can grab a Sweeper and head back."

I nod in agreement and shift to Vance who is still standing right beside me. "Alright, kid. Now you can sit here on the train and wait for your stop. You'll be able to live freely," I explained.

But Vance was already shaking his head, "I want to stay with you. I want to help you."

I laughed, "Kid, I don't want you to get hurt. It's too dangerous."

"I know, but I won't be able to feel free while the Academy is still there," he said confidently.

I have no other words to say. His statement is something I could not argue with. I didn't want Vance to get involved or get hurt. But the longer I thought about it, the more I thought about Laura. The bravery and the loyalty in Vance that he shows just causes me to think of her and what she would want to do.

I am reluctant, I sigh and I curse, "Damnit, kid. Just don't get involved with the fighting, you hear me?"

Vance nodded, "As long I'm with you I won't need to fight."

I laughed, "Good. Now, we need to get off this train."

Kenneth started walking towards the front of the train and said, "I'm on it, councilman."

In a matter of seconds, the train slows down, making the wheels grind on the rails, releasing a screeching sound. The train engine huffs and puffs until the whole thing comes to a stop.

I look to Jeffrey, who is still sitting paranoid in the front seat, and says, "Thank you for everything, Jeffrey. I wish you good luck on your travels." Jeffrey said nothing and waved at me goodbye in complete shock.

Vance and I walk to the front of the train and hop out with Kenneth, who is already waiting for us on the ground. As we touch the ground, the train begins to turn its wheels and continue its journey through the woods. Now there was the hike back to the Academy. No turning back now.

# ROBINS

The sound of the train whistle and its wheels grinding on the rails began to soften as it grew farther and farther away from us. Now the sound of wind blowing into the trees and bushes is the only thing roaming the air along with the sounds of our footsteps crushing the leaves beneath us.

Kenneth was the first to speak, "Councilman, I apologize again for what happened back there. I didn't know about the false bounty, I was just following orders."

"Please, just Robins is fine, no more Councilman. And don't worry about it, you're here now and you're helping me make it right," I reassured. "Sorry about your face, by the way," I apologized.

Kenneth chuckled, "That's alright, Councilman . . . I mean . . . Robins . . . sir. I've learned to take a beating."

I begin to take a liking to this man. He didn't seem too phased by the damage that he had taken. That meant he was trained well.

"How many bounties have you acquired, Kenneth?" I asked.

"Six, sir. Still fairly new at this job. I've only been active for about a year," Kenneth responded.

"Six, huh? That's not bad. Very good, actually. Usually Hunters would reach their second or third by the time they finish their first year," I explained.

"Thank you, sir. I've actually been wanting to be like you for a time. I was inspired by your story about the Great Storm Chase," he said, excited.

I laughed, "Damn, what a trip that was. I didn't know you knew about that."

"Well of course, sir. Almost everyone knows about that story."

"What's the Great Storm Chase?" Vance asked, finally jumping in the conversation.

I look at him, "Oh that's a story for another time. A long one in fact. In short, it was my most famous bounty hunt. Took me weeks to track down my bounty all the way through

Tornado Alley. It wasn't called that back then, but I was able to go through some of the biggest storms there and capture my bounty," I said.

"How many bounties have you acquired, Robins?" Kenneth asked.

I sighed, not really knowing the answer to the question. "Too many to count. Well over fifty before I became Councilman, that's for sure. I wasn't really too proud of all of them though." My smile slowly started to drift into a frown. "Some of those people that I hunted weren't exactly bad people, you see," I began to explain.

"Some of those people had families. They did wrong in order to help some of their own that were suffering. I didn't know what their true intentions were and I didn't know their perspective. All I knew was I had a job and I needed to accomplish it. So, once I had accomplished my mission, it was already too late when I found out what they were doing."

There was silence between all of us. The others looked like they didn't know how to respond. So I continued, "That's why I became Councilman. In order to place bounties on the people that were truly and intentionally trying to hurt others, to hurt society."

"I didn't know, sir. I'm sorry," Kenneth said.

I shook my head, "It's not your fault. I wanted to do something good, but ever since I-" I swallowed, struggling to say what I had in mind.

I began to think about Laura, my best friend who had passed

because of something that the Academy ordered upon her. Once again, my rage begins to build up and my face becomes hot. My knuckles turned white as I rolled them into fists.

Then, Vance places his hand on my back and looks me in the eyes. His gaze seemed to drain the angry energy from my system and release it. Looking upon him made my body calm down and finally I was able to recollect my thoughts.

I take a deep breath, "I lost my best friend a few years ago. She was part of the Academy, a Hunter in fact. But, she had other morals that the Academy didn't understand. They placed a bounty on her and murdered her, not giving her a chance to explain herself or even give her a fair trial."

I feel pain filling my stomach. "She was the only one that understood me at the time. She was the only one to support me," I said, swallowing my sorrows.

"Robins, we will avenge her. We will find who is placing these bounties and we will extinguish them," said Kenneth, trying to make me feel better.

"Look, we're almost there," Vance then said, pointing forward towards the camp which is not more than a hundred yards from us.

All of a sudden, I hear movement to our left in the brush. I stop both Vance and Kenneth and peer deep into the forest, searching for any sign of movement. I stare into the dense forest, into the piles of leaves, the mesh of sticks and branches. Nothing moved, everything is still. At first I thought it might've been a rodent of some sort.

Then I see a pair of eyes, staring straight at me in a bush

near a tree just about twenty feet from us. I keep my eyes on them and realize it is him. It is David, the boy I placed the bounty on. He is frozen, petrified like he's looking at the devil. He must've hated me for the last couple of days, must be terrified, and I deserve it.

I looked at Vance and Kenneth and said, "It's nothing, just keep walking. I'll be right behind you."

"You sure it's alright, sir?" Kenneth asked.

I nodded, "Yes, just go. I'll look around for a second."

Kenneth and Vance walk towards the camp while I stay behind, still looking at David. I nod at David, not really knowing what to do or say. He already seems frightened and I don't want him to feel worse. It was better that he continues running while he has the chance.

I ran to catch up with Kenneth and Vance to the camp, which we now can see in the clearing. We walk towards the left building and open the door to reveal a half destroyed room with a car sitting inside that decimated the wall. The left part of the room was intact with radios and screens.

I turn on one of the radios sitting on a desk, which is mainly to contact the Academy or other Hunters in the field. At first I wanted to contact the Academy in order to find information about who is authorizing the bounties. As I turn the dial to the same station as the Academy, causing static noises to come out, the station locks.

I speak into the mic, "HQ, this is Councilman Robins. Do you read?"

The other line takes a second, but a second person responds,

"HQ to Councilman Robins, we read you. We have information about David Conrack."

My face went pale and I am almost afraid to ask the next question, "What information do you have?"

The line hesitated again, "We are certain that he will be spotted soon and have a location as to where we can meet him. The Hunters will be approaching him shortly at White Rapid Park."

This information makes me nauseous, knowing that David might not be able to get away from this. Once a location is set, it is almost impossible for a bounty to get away. At this point, I knew I couldn't do anything about it.

# DAVID

'm petrified, confused, astonished, so many emotions flow through my head. When I saw Robins stare me down, I thought I was dead. I thought that he would've chased after me, strangled me, and eventually killed me. But he just walked away, not saying a word to me. I didn't know why.

"Why didn't he just attack us?" I asked Linda. "I mean, he put the bounty on me. He wanted me dead, right?"

Linda looked as confused as I was, "I don't know. Maybe he turned over a new leaf in the last day and a half?"

"It doesn't make sense. One day he wanted me dead, and now he's letting me go?" I questioned.

"Maybe we should take advantage of it and keep moving. We're getting close to the mountains anyways," Linda suggested.

I nodded, "You're right, I don't want to stay here much longer."

I grab my crutch and stand up on my one good and uninjured leg. I grunt in pain as I get out of the bush. Linda supported me, making sure that I wouldn't fall accidentally. Eventually I was standing on my right leg with my left holding hardly any weight with the toes touching the ground.

"Are you alright?" Linda asked.

I exhaled, "I'm alright, let's get moving."

We press on towards our destination, which seems to be growing larger and closer. Linda was right, we are getting close. Hope begins to sink into my body and my blood rushes, making me want to walk faster. Or limp for that matter.

"David, maybe you should slow down a bit," Linda said.

"I'm fine, I just want to get to those mountains," I said.

"I know that, but you should pace yourself before you fall."

"I said I'm fine, we need to get there as soon as poss-" I get no further as my crutch gets caught on a root, causing me to tumble onto my injured arm. I grunt in pain once again, not just from the fall but the surging agony throughout my right arm.

Linda quickly kneels down to help and sits me up. "You're stupid, you know that?" she scolded.

I sigh in embarrassment and annoyance. "Why did you come out here, Linda?"

"What do you mean?" she asked, looking concerned.

"I mean, why did you come all this way? Throwing everything you worked for and risking your whole life just for me?"

She took a second to collect her thoughts on how to respond. "What I worked for was not for me, I didn't have a choice and neither did you. I threw away my slavery so that I may have a real life," she said.

I didn't know how to respond, she said her sentence with such passion that it stunned me. Her eyes are filled with anger for having been a servant for the Academy for so long. But yet, I still get a sense of hope from her, saying that she may be able to get away from it after all.

The next thing that I knew, Linda was leaning in towards my face and holding it with her soft hand. "Maybe I could have a real life with you," she said softly. She then closed her eyes, leaned in closer and pressed her lips against mine.

My heart pounded and my cheeks burned up, I felt as if I'm in a dream, like I'm kissing a princess. She lets go from her kiss and looks at me with her beautiful, ocean blue eyes. I couldn't look away because of how pretty she is. I feel like the luckiest man on the planet.

"Well . . . er . . . um . . . I better get you to that camp so that you may be safe," I said now smiling with complete and utter joy.

Linda giggled, "You won't do much with those wounds."

"It's alright, I'm feeling much better now," I said, of course now that I just kissed the girl of my dreams.

I quickly stand up with my crutch once again, still feeling the surging pain throughout my arm, leg and face. At this point though, I shrug off the pain and put a little more pressure on my bad leg.

I point and begin to limp, with confidence. "Alright, let's get to that camp!" I said.

In my heart, I'm excited and more hopeful to reach those mountains. In my mind though, I knew we weren't done with our journey yet.

# 22

## DAVID

We're able to walk for longer than I thought with the injuries I have to deal with. I'm able to put a lot more weight on my left leg after walking for about half an hour. We got far enough to reach White Rapid Park, which is the next place that Linda predicted we would reach.

The terrain is more mountainous, the ground is more rocky and there are fewer patches of grass. The park is spacious, with a large and very narrow ravine running towards the mountains that has a bridge going across it. There are sets of trails that run in various directions, one is to our right that seems to be the entrance and across the ravine to the left is going to an unknown location. There is a swing set directly in front towards the back near the other sets of trees and a carousel in the middle. A jungle gym and monkey bars are to the right of the swing set and a bench sits looking towards the ravine.

The day starts turning to dusk and the storm clouds are getting closer towards us. The wind blows a cold breeze and the sun hardly keeps an orange light going in the sky. The air smelled of dirt and algae, mainly coming from the ravine.

Linda and I walk towards the bench to take a break. I sit down quite swiftly without causing any pain to my injuries.

"So, what do you think we'll do once we get to the Runaways?" I asked.

"I don't know, there's nothing much to expect. Maybe they'll get us through the mountains to live a normal life," Linda responded.

I snorted playfully, "More walking, sounds like a dream."

Linda gazes at me with annoyance and slaps me softly on my right knee, smiling.

I laughed, "What? It just seems like more work."

Linda brought her eyebrows together and her jaw dropped, "You've worked in the hot and humid pipeline your whole life and you're complaining about more work?"

"You know I'm joking, right?" I asked with a huge grin on my face.

Linda rolled her eyes and smiled knowing that I was purposefully pulling her leg.

"I wonder how many people escaped and how many are at that camp," Linda says.

I look up to the mountains, hoping to see a light or some indication that there is a camp up there. "I don't know, but I hope there is some sweets and hot chocolate," I said thinking of the hot and delectable beverage with white and chewy marshmallows floating on the top.

"Mmm, that'll be the day," Linda agreed.

"Well then, let's waste no time. Let's get that hot chocolate," I said getting up.

Linda smiled and jumped up, readying herself for the rest of the walk up the mountain.

Suddenly, I hear a voice from across the park towards the entrance say, "There they are!!" My eyes dart towards the noise and I see a few Sweepers roll up with Rippers getting out of each one. The most frightening part is that I could hear more cars driving towards us coming from the trails. The ones on foot look tired, but are doing everything they could to catch us and begin to sprint in our direction.

I drop my crutch, putting my full weight on both my legs and grab Linda's hand to pull her towards the mountains. We run towards the mountains as fast as we can, following the ravine.

Then I had a crazy idea. Since they have their Sweepers, we couldn't outrun them. There are too many for us to handle, we could barely handle two. There is no other cover for us to get behind. Except for the ravine.

I pull Linda towards the bridge in front of us. I knew I was not going to like this idea and she wasn't going to either.

We are about fifty meters from the bridge when Linda yells, "What are you doing?!"

"Just trust me! It's the only way!" I yell back, now twenty meters away.

"You're crazy!" Linda responded.

Ten meters now and I can just feel the Rippers edging closer and closer to us, ready to snatch us.

I scream, "Jump!" as we reach the bridge, push off the platform and over the rail. It takes my breath away and now we are plunging ourselves into what looked to be a thirty foot drop into the running water.

# DAVID

I t felt like it took several moments to reach the rapidly moving water at the bottom of the ravine. Luckily, the water is deep enough for us to survive the fall. However, the impact of the water courses through my legs and weakens my injured leg again.

As I plunge into the water, the current immediately takes me with it. I swim upwards, desperately searching for air. I'm able to poke my head out to the surface, but the waves are tossing my body around like a ragdoll. The freezing water flows towards the mountains downhill.

I could see Linda a little further upstream, trying to keep her head above the water.

"Linda!" I screamed, getting a mouthful of water.

Linda looks back at me trying to swim against the current towards me.

"Grab a rock!" I scream, getting another large mouthful of water.

She seemed to understand as she moved to the right, desperately trying to cling onto a large rock. She reaches for a few, but the current pushes her past them, not giving her time to latch on. After several tries, she manages to hold onto one off to the side near the wall of the ravine.

She looks at me and holds out her hand to reach for me as I flow with the waves rapidly. I push the water, moving closer and closer in her direction and reach as far as my arm will go. We lock hands and Linda pulls me in behind the rock, still holding onto it.

Linda then pulls me into a hug, squeezing one another. I hold onto the rock as well to prevent myself from going down the stream.

"Are you alright?" I asked.

"I should be asking you that," she responded, looking down at my leg engulfed in the water. It's leaking blood that is getting sucked up by the stream once it gets past our rock.

"I'm fine. Let's just make it down to the end of the stream before we freeze."

"Good plan," Linda said.

All of a sudden, the rock shakes as a crashing noise of metal on rock is heard upstream. A Sweeper is heading in our direction by driving through the rapids, followed by a second one falling all the way down behind it which caused a second crash. The car itself didn't seem to make a dent or even show any damage.

"Go now!" I screamed.

Both of us let go of the rock and start swimming downstream. I paddle and push as much as I can, stressing out my injured right shoulder. The sound of the cars bouncing up and down gets closer and louder every second. My breath was stagnant from using all the energy I could to get away and gasping for air.

I knew there had to be something we could do and it wasn't going to be swimming away. We couldn't fight them, especially in water, because we would be killed on the spot. We could hide, but there was a good chance they'll know the general area of where we are. There seemed to be no way out as we traveled further and further down this ice cold river.

There is a way to make it look like they got us. That involved both hiding and the bleeding injury that I had. I have to get Linda with me first, who is still fairly close to me.

"Find another rock!" I screamed, grabbing her by her side.

We push ourselves to the side once again, reaching for another rock, trying not to faceplant into it. The crashing noise is louder than ever, as if they are just about to run us over. My adrenaline rushes through my heart and my limbs are exhausted. I could hardly push any further.

As I feel the wheels of the Sweeper inching closer, Linda grabs another rock and swings us behind it and I yell, "Dive!"

We sink into the water as the bottom part of the car slices right through the surface of the water, nearly taking off our heads. Once I knew that the Sweeper passed us and we were secure, I smashed my injury with my fist as hard as I could to release more blood repeatedly.

The pain was excruciating, I could hardly hold my breath. Then the second Sweeper began to drive over us. The wheels crash in the water so close to our heads that I could have kissed it most likely.

I hold Linda down in the water to keep us from being spotted. I know we had to be in the clear in a few seconds after they looked around as they left. As I am about to run out of air, I pull Linda up and myself above the surface for air. I look downstream seeing nothing but a fork in the ravine, the rapids, and the back end of the Sweeper heading towards the left.

"We did it!" I yell, and I gaze over at Linda who is holding her head. "Linda? Are you alright? Are you hurt?"

"Yeah, let's just get to the end," she said, seeming to be in pain.

"Just hold on," I said, grasping her while we headed downstream once again.

I carefully bob and weave away from any incoming rocks, protecting Linda and her injured head. It didn't seem to be bleeding, which is a good sign I believe. However she didn't look like she was doing well, she seemed dazed and wasn't too phased by any of the splashes.

The waves calms down as we go right, the opposite direction of the Sweepers. The stream dies down into a pond that sits right below the mountains. Not many trees grow around here and the only thing I see looking forward is the rocks of the mountains going upward.

I lead Linda to the shoreline, who doesn't seem to be moving at all. I drag her out of the cold water into the winter breeze, which isn't good at all. She lays on her back, not moving a muscle. Her eyes are closed but she's still breathing as I check and see if her chest is still rising.

"Linda? Can you hear me?" I said, now becoming scared that I might lose her, the girl that is willing to risk everything for me. The one who I fell in love with, the one that would look after me. I couldn't lose her, not now.

I look around for any kind of shelter as the breeze begins to pick up. There is nothing around that I could use, nothing for me to do in order to help her. The Rippers are still behind us so I couldn't go back. I didn't have anything dry that could help her. There is nothing.

The only thing I see is the mountains standing higher than the storm clouds racing towards us, which sends flakes of snow down to us and starts to get even more harsh.

## ROBINS

The smell of oil and gasoline fills the air in the garage and workshop of the Academy camp. Two rows of three Sweepers are parked in this area with one Sweeper showing signs of a struggle such as a scratch in the paint and the passenger door open. Lying next to it is a dead Hunter that has his neck cut. Past him is his partner lying with his back against the wall with blood seeping through his chest.

I stay away from the bodies and move to one of the

untouched cars, grabbing the keys hung up on the wall. I open the driver seat door when Kenneth walks in.

"Sir, if you don't mind me asking, why were you surprised when they announced that Conrack was about to be captured?" Kenneth asked.

I sighed, "I didn't want him to be captured and especially killed. I never wanted him harmed."

"So, was it another false bounty?" Kenneth wondered.

I shook my head, "No, this one was on me. I announced that large bounty."

"So then, why did you do it if you didn't want him to be hurt?"

I looked up at him after opening the Sweeper, "I was angry at the time. And if you heard, I don't deal with anger very well," I began. "But, I wanted the Academy gone and still do because of what they do to people and families. I was planning to have David help me extinguish it by setting up explosives. But again, I was angry and couldn't control it. So, when the alarm went off and the plan failed, I lost all control and um . . . I tried to get rid of anyone who would know what I was trying to do," I explained, thinking back on my mistakes.

I hesitated, getting choked up on my words. "I killed good people that day, officers in fact. I regret it all. Especially the bounty on David, who is also a victim of what I did. Vance was a victim, too. I couldn't let him die because of my limitations," I said. "All I want to do is free the people who have fallen victim to the Academy. I hope you can understand what this is about and hope you can understand me."

Kenneth walks over to me, "Sir, you are trying to help people. I am one of the people who have fallen victim to the Academy. All I wanted was to be set free, of course I understand you."

I smiled at him, "Thank you."

Kenneth smiles back and then immediately claps his hands together, "So, what's the plan, boss?"

My smile drifts away, I didn't think about what was to come next. "I'm not sure. I can't take down the Academy by myself and certainly not with just us three. We need more people to get involved."

"What about the Runaways? The people who have escaped the Academy," Kenneth suggested.

I thought about it, "It would be possible. Rumors were spread that they are planning something against the Academy. But I would need to get in contact and I don't know who I would go to."

We sit in silence, trying to come up with some idea as to who we would be able to talk to.

"There's got to be someone in the Academy itself," Vance said, already through the doorway. "If there is a rumor that I have heard it's that there is someone in the Pipeline that is giving information about the Runaways. That's why I never really talked to anyone there at the time."

Then I obtain a clue as to who it might be. There were only a few people that David talked to that I didn't think about until now and that was his close group of friends. The skinny-freckled face boy, the dark skinned young man and his buddy, the short and pale one. I don't know names but I know faces.

One of them must be the one to give David information to the Runaways once he got out of the police station.

"Kid, well done," I said to Vance. He smiles with more joy than I have ever seen him have.

I ran towards the armory and training facility, which is the next building over. I go through the hallway so fast as if it wasn't even there. I push through the double doors and reach for two sets of blades. Immediately I ran back to the garage with the same amount of speed, coming back in less than thirty seconds.

"Kenneth, get ready. Get backpacks and supplies from medical and survival," I call Kenneth.

He nods and runs through the other set of double doors. I move quickly to the Sweeper I opened and type into the keypad numbers 5223, my master code for these Sweepers in particular. The car was ready to go as the lights turned on the inside for the radio and more.

"Hey, kid," I said, gesturing to Vance to come closer.

He obeys and walks right in front of me. "Listen, I admire how much you are committed to this and how braver you have become. I just want you to know that no matter what happens during this plan, if I don't come back, you keep going. Do you understand me?"

"But, you will come back right?" Vance asked, concerned.

I give him a smile, "I will do my best, kid. The important thing is that you live on. You have a whole life ahead of you. You need to live."

Vance then lunges in for a hug, wrapping his arms around

my neck and squeezing. I hesitate and slowly hug him back, almost not knowing what to do.

"You will come back," Vance said.

Vance let go of his grapple, showing sheds of tears. But they are not tears of sadness. They are tears of hope and joy.

Kenneth burst through the double doors saying, "I think we're ready, sir! I gotta say, I've never been more excited!"

# 25

## ROBINS

Kenneth begins driving the Sweeper through the forest towards the Academy. The ground bounces the car up and down countless times and the branches and bushes get pummeled by the sheer amount of force the automobile delivers. The bouncing doesn't seem to go well with Vance as he appears like a zombie sitting in the back seat.

"So what's the plan, boss?" Kenneth asked, recklessly driving through the brush.

"We need to find one of David's friends in the pipeline. One of them has to know how to contact the Runaways. If we can get them to tell us or show us, then we'll be able to have enough people to raid the Academy at night. I'll explain more if we get that far," I explained.

"We'll get that far," Kenneth said confidently.

The Sweeper drives up a large hill, working hard up this steep ramp. It isn't too hard of a job for the armored car and it manages to scale the climb, leaving behind a large tire mark in the dirt.

Above the hill reveals Lone Camp, a small town that was meant to be an indication of the Academy camp sitting next to it. Kenneth slams the gas, moving us past the town with incredible speed. The motor roars as the car slides through the trees once again, heading for the next town over which is where the Academy is.

"Once we get back, keep the Sweeper close and running. We'll need to move as quickly as possible," I told Kenneth, who nodded.

"What about me?" Vance asked from behind the seat.

I looked back, "You're going to stay with Kenneth, alright?"

"Why can't I come?" he asked.

"Because you might get spotted by one of the Hunters again, we can't have that happen. You would be in the direct center of it all."

"Aren't most of the Hunters after David anyway?"

I open my mouth to respond and then I realize what Vance was saying.

He continued, "If most of them are after him, then the Academy would be more vulnerable. And if I stay by you they won't mess around. Plus, you might need someone who can vouch for you."

Vance was correct, the Hunters are out there looking for David, a bounty that I initiated with very high value as a matter of fact. He's probably worth more than $100,000. Normally a bounty would be around a thousand to about ten thousand. Since he is worth so much, almost all the Hunters in the Academy are looking for him.

With that being said, the Academy doesn't have many people protecting it at the moment. So the raid would do nicely.

Vance was also correct when he said he could vouch for me. It's true that any Runaway would probably hate me because of all the bounties being released, especially the false ones that are being blamed on me.

I looked over at Kenneth, who is still booking it back to the Academy. He glances at me quickly, noticing that I was staring at him.

"Don't look at me. The kid's got a point," he said, focusing on the drive.

I peer back at Vance, who is once again giving the dog eyes. I snarled, "Damnit, kid. Why do you always win?"

I look forward through the windshield and notice that we are already back in town. I hadn't paid attention to Kenneth's driving for a bit, I must've missed everything going by. He wasn't messing around when he floored the gas.

Kenneth slows down, driving on the streets and safely

passing cars all around. We turn corners from left to right and in a short period of time I can see the large, factory-like building that was the Academy.

Kenneth turns into the driveway and parks off to the side of the Academy. Once we stop, I quickly get out of the car with Vance coming out behind me.

"Stay close to me," I say to Vance.

"As always," he responds.

I give a grin at that response and open the double doors into the building. The space seems more filled even with the lacking number of Hunters. Workers with documents, tools and other materials walk all around the building, especially going towards the pipeline.

Some people gaze over to me and Vance. Some give smiles, greeting me back to the workplace. Others just give a nod and walk away. None paid much attention to Vance walking right beside me, which was a very good sign. We head straight for the pipeline, which is crowded with people going through the door and surrounded by guards who wore their own set of blades.

It's a slow walk down the few steps to take into the hot and humid room. Workers are constantly crafting at the workstations, using blow torches and hammers to mainly make blades. The pipes are filled with workers, consistently making sure everything was working perfectly and some even working on leaks. The guards stood around the room, constantly checking the room.

I search the room for anyone in David's close group of friends. It is hard to tell who is who since lots have their backs turned or even have facewear on. I walk further into the room, getting a closer look at anyone that seems familiar.

Finally, towards the electrical systems, is the skinny and freckled faced fellow. I couldn't remember his name. *Tanner? Larry?* I can't remember. All I know is that is the person that David would talk most to.

As I walk closer to him, he turns to me and gives a disgusted look.

"Councilman, is there something I can help you with?" he asked.

"Yes actually. Um . . . Randy is it?" I asked for confirmation.

"Connor, sir," he corrected, giving a sour look.

"Connor, of course. Listen . . . I need to know where David went," I said, not knowing how to start the conversation.

"I thought you had him on the run, sir," he said, giving an even fiercer look.

"Look, I'm trying to help him and I need to know where he went so that he may live. I know you must feel indifferent about me saying this, but we need to take down this place so that more people like him can live freely," I explained as best I could in a softer tone to avoid others from hearing.

"Please, you have to help us," Vance chimed in.

Connor glances over at Vance, almost puzzled. He looks closely until his eyes widen, "You're . . . you're that kid that was executed," he said in such shock.

"Robins saved me and he wants to do the same for others. You have to trust him. You're our only hope of defeating the Academy and saving David," Vance said.

Connor sighs, looking at both of us with much thought. He looks down and sighs much more deeply than the last one. His head rises up and peers past us, "Mike, Roger. Come over here," he called.

Behind us the dark boy and the short pale boy walks over towards us, still holding their tools. The dark boy held a wrench while the other held a flathead screwdriver.

They both gave the same looks that Connor was giving me earlier.

"Tell them where Roy is," Connor told them.

The dark one, I believe was Mike, made a physical reaction, backing away and making a very concerned face. "Why?" he asked.

"They're trying to help David, just do it," Connor responded reluctantly.

Mike turned to me, looked back at Connor, then back to me. "Weiland and Harrison Clothing Shop, go there and someone will tell you all you need to know," he said, seeming like it almost killed him to say it.

"Thank you, boys. It'll help David, I promise you," I said. "Oh and please get yourselves and everyone else out of here soon. It might not be here tomorrow."

The three of them give surprised and confused looks, especially at one another. I gesture to Vance to get out of the building, glad that we got some information. I sigh with relief.

We quickly move past all the people coming in, out of the pipeline, and out of the main entrance to the building. The Sweeper that Kenneth is sitting in is still running like I told him to. Both of us quickly get back in the car with Vance in the back seat once again.

"So where are we headed, sir?" Kenneth asked excitedly.

"We're going to a clothing shop, Kenneth," I responded.

## 26

### ROBINS

Rain starts to trickle down onto the windshield and the wind picks up so much it seems to move the car. The sky becomes dark as the storm clouds roll over the mountains and are soaring through the air right towards us faster than a train. Darkness is engulfing the town at this point.

"A clothing shop? Really?" Kenneth asked with such annoyance.

"What's wrong, Kenneth? What happened to that excitement I was hearing before?" I said, playing with his lack of enthusiasm.

"Well . . . I thought there would be something else, sir."

"Like what? A secret tunnel leading into a labyrinth full of talking monkeys?" I laughed.

Kenneth didn't respond, looking more irritated now than enthusiastic. As we drive, I tell him to turn to the left towards the A&P store where I left the gang members. Of course, they weren't there anymore and they must've had a rough night.

The clothing shop, Weiland and Harrison Clothing, is sitting a few stores down the road and on the other side of the street from the A&P store. I tell Kenneth to park right on the curb and he does so without hesitation. I realize that this is the same place that we went to get Vance new clothes.

A light is still on from the inside of the shop and as we get out of the car into the rain that is now coming down harder, I knock with much force. It takes a few seconds for a shadow to appear through the window and for them to open the door.

"I'm sorry, sir, but we're closed f'r the day," an old man responded.

"Roy, is it? Are you the man who has been helping the Runaways?" I asked.

The old man frowned, "Depends who's askin'."

"Someone who wants the Academy gone," I responded with some aggression.

The old man huffs and opens the door wider to allow us into the building. The shop is just like how I remember it with more to see from the last time I was here since it was dark. I could see more options for clothing such as hats and accessories and a set of stairs going up with a chandelier hanging at the top.

"Are ya fellers Runaways?" Roy asked.

"No, I am a councilman, I'm councilman Robins. This is Kenneth who is a former hunter now and this is Vance. We need help from you to take down the Academy," I explained.

"Ah, I see. So you're the one that announces them bounties, are ya?"

"Well, yes but-" I began and got no further as he cut me off.

"So then why would I help ya? You sendin' those Rippers after us. F'r all I know, you could be leadin' us into a trap," he said with so much anger, eyebrows narrowing.

I have no response, this man doesn't want to believe that I want to help and there is nothing much I can do. I'm a councilman, so there is no proof that I have that could convince him that we are trying to be on his side.

"Please, sir, you have to believe us," Vance chimed in. "The bounties are being initiated by someone else. We know what the Academy has done and we want to end it.

"It's true, I will have no part of the Academy anymore," Kenneth added and began taking his blades off his arm and dropping them at Roy's feet.

Vance followed suit as well as myself, unstrapping the blades on my right arm. Roy looks down at the blades, stunned by what our actions showed. A Hunter never reveals his blades until ready, and most certainly does not give up his blades. Giving up the blades shows a great deal of trust or surrender.

Roy looks up at us and says, "Y'all are serious?"

"As serious as a stab wound," I responded.

Roy hesitates for a second and immediately beckons us to follow him in the back room. This room is small, only showing a table in the middle and a desk to the left where a radio is sitting. The right wall contains a map of the town and more, the landscape, nearby cities and towards the mountains. Several lines were drawn throughout the map leading to a spot in the mountains. The lines went past Lone Camp and the railroad tracks sometimes through them.

"What're y'all planning, huh?" Roy asked.

"We need your people to help break into the facility. Help us get into the pipeline so that we can set up gasoline, get everyone out and blow the whole thing straight to hell. There won't be too many Hunters there since they are after a large bounty, so we have a window of opportunity," I explained.

Roy nodded across the table, "Alright, but I have ta ask. Why're you suddenly helpin' us? I thought you was loyal to the Academy."

I begin to think about why I am doing this, for my best friend Laura. Thinking about her isn't causing me to go into a blind rage, it only makes my eyes tear up.

"I had a friend in the Academy, and she was killed by them. She was innocent and I don't want that happening to anyone else ever again," I said, trying to keep my voice straight.

# 27

## DAVID

Snow falls from the storm clouds, the wind blows through the trees, and down the mountain. The sun is completely blocked by the storm that blew in and is now covering every inch of the ground with snow. There is nothing around to protect us, not many trees are around here.

I try waking up Linda, who is still lying motionless on the ground soaked in her jacket. I begin to shiver due to the cold and the temperature is only going to decrease at this point. I try to think of something to do, a way out of this situation.

There's nothing but the mountain, which appears like our only hope of surviving both the Rippers and the environment. I glance down at Linda once again, trying one last time to wake her up by saying her name and touching her face. There's no response, only very light breathing.

I curse under my breath after I realize that there is only one way out of this, and that is scaling the mountain towards the Runaway camp. I waste no more time, I sit up Linda, and get in front of her to pick her up on my back. As I get my hands under her thighs and lift with my legs, the searing pain comes back throughout my left calf. I wince at the pain, but still push with all the force I would need.

I rotate towards the mountain and I begin to walk. Having Linda on my back helps a little with the low temperatures. Although, the pain in my leg and shoulder are the main concern. Every step is sending a wave of agony through one or the other.

I carefully plant my foot in the rocks, making sure that the rock is secure and there is not a lot of ice to slip on. The number of trees decreased and the snow became harsher every step of the way up. The snow feels like shards of glass slicing at my face, tearing off the bandages.

Still, I keep pushing onwards up the mountain. Rock after rock I step over, pushing as hard as I can against the ground as I could to keep myself and Linda up. One wrong step and we could tumble all the way down. That wasn't something I wanted to think about. I don't look down nor turn around to check how far I've gone. All I care about is making it to that camp and fast.

My body aches, especially my leg that is bleeding through the bandages and becoming worse each step of the way. I don't care though, I want to make it. I want to live, I want Linda to live. My leg and shoulder throbs and burns even though it is astoundingly cold.

More and more the storm picks up and the snow turns it into a blizzard. Almost nothing is visible, I could barely look at the steps that I am taking through all the precipitation in my sight. My body shivers and the one thing that I'm hoping not to happen begins to happen.

I take a step with my right foot and suddenly I slip, losing my balance in the snow and rocks. I try catching myself with my injured leg, but the pain is too much and I fall towards my right side. I am brought down to my knees and my grip of Linda left me as she tumbles to the side as well.

Everything in my body is freezing, I shiver and stiffen. There isn't much energy left inside that could go on. This storm is too much, the pain is too much and the thought of not being able to make it to the camp is too much.

I look at Linda lying in the snow. She is still unconscious, but her lips are blue. A very bad sign that Linda might be close to freezing to death. Her skin is paler than ever and her breathing is almost unnoticeable.

I look up, desperately searching for some sort of sign that we might be close to the camp. The wind and snow blows fiercely into my face, and I can barely open my eyes. I search around, not seeing any source of a camp. Just the white blanket of snow and rocks. It's over, there is nothing else, we're going to die here.

But then, I see a tiny light up ahead towards the right. I lift my head up as I have refueled my hope in my heart. I quickly begin to pick up Linda once again, this time by carrying her in my arms in front. I scream in pain as I lift her up, not having much fuel in me to go on.

I'm so tired, especially from all the running in the recent past. My body wants to shut down and my eyes become droopy. It seems like I'm going to fall asleep. A rest sounds nice I thought. But no, I need to keep moving and I shake my head awake to keep walking.

But my eyes immediately begin to close and I shake my head again to stay awake. I couldn't give up, not when we're so close. All I want is to get Linda to safety, I want her to live the life that she deserves. I push with everything that I have left, screaming at the top of my lungs for help.

The light is brighter now, but there is no movement coming from the source. I scream again, pushing just a little bit further. However, my legs and arms couldn't take it anymore. My legs collapse from underneath me and I drop Linda in front of me into the snow. I try moving towards her, but my limbs are unable to allow me to move. I'm freezing and aching. My eyes become droopy once again and this time close shut and my mind goes black.

# DAVID

Suddenly my body begins to feel warm once again, all around my face mostly. I must be dead is what I'm thinking. But I open my eyes, very slowly as they are sore from the wind pounding in my eye sockets. To the right of me is a light, a very bright light in fact. It's a flame, I notice, since the light was moving. Although I couldn't move myself, I felt constricted.

I open my eyes more and look down at myself. I'm lying down on my back and wrapped in a sleeping bag, along with blankets on the inside. Looking up I see just a rocky ceiling, I'm in a cave of some sort. Looking around I could see large tents set up, other campfires with pots hung up on poles to cook the contents inside. People are walking around in coats, some are bandaged and some lying down in a sleeping bag as well. Some sit in their own makeshift and folded chairs.

My head is swimming, I'm still recovering from the storm. I'm confused and don't know where I am. Then I start to think about Linda. *Where was she? Was she alive? Is she here with me?* I open my eyes completely and turn my body over to see that she is right next to me, right by my head where she lay there still unconscious. Her head is wrapped in bandages and her lips are no longer blue, but her face is still pale.

"Oh, you're awake!" a voice said from behind my head.

It's a woman sitting in her own seat wrapped in a fur coat. She has many freckles on her face and her brown hair is short that dangled right above her shoulders. She put her hand on my forehead like she was checking for temperature.

"Much better than when we found you. When you got here you guys were as cold as ice. Now you just feel like melting ice cream," she said with a smile.

"Where are we?" I asked.

"Oh, you're at the Runaway camp. Roy said you'd be showing up here. Let me tell you, you're both lucky to be alive. Otherwise that storm would've gobbled you up like a bunch of hungry lions," she answered. "I'm Sandra, by the way."

"Nice to meet you, I'm David and that's Linda," I said, starting to sit up.

"Oh easy now, not too fast," she suggested, bringing her hands on my back to support me. "I'll get you some supper."

Sandra walks away towards one of the pots and grabs a bowl and spoon. She pours the contents into the bowl with a bigger spoon and immediately walks back towards us. At this point I'm able to pull out my arms, feeling sore but warm from all the blankets.

"Here's your hot bowl of soup, order up," she said.

She hands me the steaming bowl of soup that smells glorious. Looking at it reveals chunks of meat, carrots, celery, and noodles. As I'm staring at the delicious bowl of soup, I also notice that I'm wearing different clothing. A nice, thick coat was zipped on me and I wore a dry set of pants.

"Um . . . where are my clothes?" I asked awkwardly.

"Oh, over there," she said, pointing towards the other side of the fire. "They're drying, so we had to give you new ones so you guys wouldn't die of hypothermia. You know, freezing to death," she explained with a smile once again.

I blush as I see my shirt and pants sitting next to the fire. I don't want to say anything, so I blow on my hot soup and take a spoonful of the delectable contents.

"Is Linda going to be alright?" I asked Sandra.

"Oh, for sure. She has a concussion and hypothermia, but she'll be alright. It looked like the concussion took her out but the cold kept her under. But, she's alright, she'll come back like a phoenix," she said confidently.

I sighed in relief and my body began to relax.

"Oh and I patched up some of your wounds, so you should

be good to go. You had some frostbite on your feet, but you're fine. The new bandages always help," Sandra added.

I laughed, "Were you a nurse at the Academy?"

"A nurse, a medic is more like it. But yes I was. That is until they started telling me I should let some of my patients die when I could've saved them. I didn't want to just let it happen, so I quit. When that happened the Rippers started to come after me. That's where I met Roy. The old man saved my life," she said.

"Wow, I'm really sorry about all that," I sympathized.

"Eh it's alright. I'm doing a hell of a lot better up here than I was at the Academy. That place was like a prison on drugs. And we had a detainment system, so I wonder what that's like," she said.

"Well, I know what a prison is like, at least for a few hours," I laughed.

She chuckled, "Oh well, it doesn't matter up here. They won't be able to find us, the Sweepers will never make it up here without wasting fuel or freezing. We're safe."

"Why not leave this place, maybe go past the mountains? Why not try to make a life somewhere else?" I asked.

"The Rippers are everywhere, they're not just within the state. Up here in the mountains is the only place we can live without them spotting us. They won't bother to check up here because they expect us to die up here. We're barely able to grab supplies from the nearby towns. That's why we can't leave, cause this is the only safe place," Sandra explained.

"Then, how would we be able to live normal lives?"

Sandra sighed, "Well, the only way would be to take down the Academy, destroy it somehow. I doubt that will happen though."

"But, I thought you guys had a plan to take down Robins and the Academy?" I asked, concerned.

Sandra shook her head, "We all thought about it. But none of us were able to find a way to beat him. He has too many supporters and we won't be able to come close to burning down that Academy."

My heart drops and my hopes fall. We came here thinking that there might have been a chance to defeat Robins and his Rippers, but now I realize that there isn't a plan at all.

At that moment, the sound of the static coming from a radio is heard coming from the big tent right behind us.

# DAVID

I get out of my sleeping bag, setting down my bowl of soup to fall in behind Sandra. The noise of the static coming from the radio attracts everyone there. They come rushing towards the tent but no one goes inside except Sandra. A voice is coming through the device saying, "Flame four . . . flame four . . . flame four . . . flame four, come in."

Sandra picks up the radio and responds with, "Cloud five, cloud five, cloud five, cloud five, we read you, Roy. Is everything alright?"

"They're more than alright, we might have a solution to that damn Academy. Somebody is here ta talk to y'all," he said.

Sandra looks back at us with a smile. Everyone around me watching her in the tent began to whisper to one another. People ask about what solution they have, some calling it unbelievable and a couple are praying.

Another voice came onto the radio, "Hello, this is Steven Robins, former councilman of the Academy. I want to help everyone who is hiding from the Hunters. But first, I'd like to know if anyone named David Conrack is there."

I'm shocked, my breath was taken away knowing that the voice was Robins and is asking for me. This is my worst nightmare, I thought. Sandra looks at me with a concerned look and gestures for me to talk into the speaker. I hesitate, shiver from the thought of Robins. My heart skips many beats as I walk into the large tent with a desk holding the radio.

I breathe in and out heavily and take the speaker, "What do you want, Robins?" I asked with much distrust.

"Look, I know I did a lot of wrong. I've put you through hell in the past few days when I didn't want to. I did those things because I was angry and I couldn't control it because of a disorder. I try coping with it but it's too much. I couldn't do anything about the bounty either, not after it was initiated. I never wanted to hurt you, I never wanted to hurt anyone there who might be listening. I apologize deeply for all the wrong that I have done," he said.

No one spoke. Everyone listening seems stunned by his words, almost not believing that this is happening.

He continued, "I know I can't take back what I have done. But what I can do is make up for it by helping everyone who has been oppressed by the Academy by tearing it down. I was trying to do this before with you, David. I was too angry at the time to explain in detail what I intended to do. But I want the Academy gone as much as all of you do. Now I know I can't be completely trusted, but I have someone here with me who would like to say something."

It is silent for a moment, only hearing the sound of the dying wind outside and the burning campfires.

"Hello, David? It's Vance, we only met for a little while. But I was supposed to be executed in public before your trial. But I was saved by Robins who helped me fake my death. I'm alive because of him and I realize now that all he wants to do is help as many people as possible. Robins is being framed by someone in the Academy who is placing false bounties and we need to stop them," he says.

I have no words to say, I can't believe that Vance is alive. My mind keeps wanting to say that this whole thing is a trap, but the more I listen to the words the more I begin to believe them.

Robins came back onto the radio, "I just want to grant everyone's lives and a chance to be free. I'm doing this because I lost my best friend to the Academy. That was your mother, David."

My eyes widen and my breath is taken away. Immediately I become confused and the tears begin to well up in my eyes just thinking about my parents.

Robins continued once again, with his voice choking up, "The Academy hunted her. She was a Hunter who fought alongside me. She was fierce, but empathetic. That's why she quit after she found out that the Academy was forcing her to take out families. They . . . " he hesitated, "They found her and your father at the ski resort and . . . and took them out."

My throat becomes sore and tears run down my face as I begin to cry.

"I'm so . . . so sorry, David. I never initiated that bounty and all I wanted to do was destroy that place once and for all. I never want that to happen to anyone else," Robins finished.

My head is swimming with emotions. Most of it is guilt for hating Robins for what he did. I didn't know that all this time he was trying to do something good for people. I feel indifferent as well because it never seemed like he was helping, only trying to hurt others is what I saw from my perspective. Then I start to miss my parents. The people that guided me, raised me, and loved me with all their hearts were gone and there was nothing I could do about it. Except for one thing.

"What plan do you have in mind?" I asked into the radio, wiping away my tears.

"I need the Runaways to help us break into and fight through the Academy. Not many Hunters will be there since they are trying to hunt you. But they won't know you're coming back. Then we need a few people to get into the pipeline using vents most likely. Once inside, they will set up propane tanks and open gas valves and unwire the electrical wiring. Once those are set up, then someone can turn on the emergency power to make the entire thing blow up straight to hell," Robins explained.

People in front of the tent became excited and began to cheer.

"Someone would have to turn on the power manually. Who's going to be willing to do that?" I asked.

"I will do that myself. I won't ask anyone else to do it. I've been waiting long enough for this moment," he said.

The people in front of the tent whisper amongst each other once again, lots of them nodding and others shaking their heads. I look over at Sandra who is sitting in the chair next to me. She looks skeptical about this plan, unsure if she wants to do it or not.

"We need to take a shot at this," I suggested.

"You really think he's telling the truth?" she asked.

I nodded, "Otherwise Vance wouldn't be alive. Roy probably never would have allowed them to speak on the radio, right?"

"I suppose," she said, still unsure.

"I think I'd rather fight for a chance to truly be free than stay isolated hoping to survive for a decent period of time."

Sandra thought about it, staring at the radio as if looking for more answers. She looks over at the rest of the people who are waiting for confirmation, standing still and silent. She stands up, walks towards them, and stops right in front of them. Everyone gazes upon her in dead silence, waiting to see what she has to say.

"Get your gear ready, you mountain dwelling goats. It's time to give them the horns!" she said, giving a wave of hope and courage.

The people cheer and begin to pack up everything they could. The people scramble around, putting up tents and grabbing weapons such as knives and even some Ripper blades. They stuff their backpacks and wait at the entrance. Some stay behind tending to the wounded and keep their campfires burning.

Linda still lay unconscious near the fire I was just at. Her color appears to come back to her and her breath is at a much more noticeable pace.

I kneel down beside her, touching her soft, warm cheek. "I'll be back. I promise," I said. The disappointing and terrifying part of that is I don't know if I am telling the truth. I have no idea what might happen next.

## ROBINS

An hour has passed, and everyone is either sitting in a chair or leaning against the wall. My adrenaline is surging and my heart is pumping rapidly, eagerly waiting to get this plan executed. I pace around the room, constantly checking the clock.

The woman on the radio said they would be there in an hour or so since they needed to pack up and get their gear down the mountain. They do have Sweepers that they stole since a few of them were Hunters themselves.

I check the clock once again to see that it is about time to get ready. "Alright, everyone. Let's move out!" I said walking out of the room.

Kenneth, Vance and Roy follow suit and fall in behind me. We walk outside into the dark where the snow stops falling and the storm has faded. The air is chilly and the streets are silent.

I turn to Vance who is walking behind me and says, "So you remember the plan, right?"

Vance nodded, "Go through the vents in the kitchen and crawl into the pipeline since the door to it is sealed shut from the inside and can't be picked and you don't have a key to it. Once I get in there, I'll open the front door before any Hunters or guards come after me."

"Good job. And don't worry about the guards, me and Kenneth will be right behind that door and we will protect you," I reassured.

"I know you will," Vance said.

"And we'll blow it all sky high afterwards," I said.

Vance's confidence suddenly turns into concern all across his face. "How will you get out if you're going to be blowing it?"

I didn't really think about it before. I don't care what is going to happen as long as the Academy is gone. Now I am thinking about it and I don't have an answer.

"I'll find a way. It'll be alright as long as that awful place is gone," I responded, trying to cheer him up.

Suddenly, Vance lunges at me with his arms wrapped around me, giving me a huge hug. "Promise you'll make it back," he said.

I hesitate, not knowing how to answer at first. I am at a loss of words. My excitement and exasperation turns into worry and guilt from not knowing if I'll be able to keep a promise like that. No one has asked me to come back to them. I almost always worked alone and never had to worry about another person except for Laura. Now I have someone to go back to, someone who truly does not want to leave my side. Now I don't want to leave him.

"I promise I'll come back," I responded, still unsure if I could keep it.

Vance lets go of me and climbs into the car. Roy stands at his shop's steps, watching us preparing for the mission.

"You're not coming?" I asked.

He shook his head, "My fightin' days 're over. Y'all know where to find me if ya need anythin'."

I nod my respects to his decision and head for the Sweeper. Kenneth is driving once again and he turns around, heading for the Academy. Roy stands watching us roll away until we couldn't see him past a corner.

It takes only a minute to get back to that unjust building. Kenneth parked in the snow, close to the building and faced the mountains. I immediately get out to unlock the trunk, which holds more supplies and extra weapons. Inside is a couple duffle bags, backpacks for survival purposes and a couple sets of blades. Some arm guards, chest plates and leg paddings made of leather are laying in here as well, enough for all three of us.

Kenneth and Vance come around to gear up as well. Kenneth starts grabbing guards that slip onto his arms and legs that he tied and strapped down. I armored up Vance with armor that is a little too big for him. At least it'll protect him, is what I thought.

After strapping him and myself into some leather padding, I grab a second set of blades that I strap to my left arm since my right was already armed. Usually, it wouldn't be ideal to put on a second set of blades. The other arm is supposed to provide leverage and support for not just the blade hand, but also environmentally. Although, I was one of the few, if not the only one to be able to fight with a second set and be effective.

Kenneth eyed the second set, "That won't be very efficient," he said.

"I'll do more damage, trust me," I responded with the most confidence.

Kenneth holds his hands in surrender, "Alright, no doubts, sir. It's just what I was taught."

Now that we are geared up and ready, all we have to do is wait for the Runaways to return to the very place they had barely escaped with their lives. History is about to be made here, I can feel it.

# ROBIN

Another hour of waiting passes as we sit in the Sweeper, waiting for the reinforcements to show up. We sit in silence, patiently waiting for the Runaways to show up and start the plan to burn down the place. We couldn't begin the operation without them since the guards would notice us in time. They seem to be more cautious now because of the failed plan that I put David and Vance through.

Suddenly, the sounds of motors roar down the streets

and lights brighten the roads and the rest of the block. Three Sweepers roll up in front of the factory-like building and park beside us. The people quickly jump out of their cars, armed and ready for a fight. There looks to be about a dozen or more people that have shown up. Then I see David come out of the second car wearing a green, air force coat.

All three of us in the Sweeper come out and come face to face with the Runaways, the people that have survived for years from the Academy. The lucky ones that managed to hide from the most elite hunters. Now they're here to take revenge, to earn their own lives for once.

I look down at David, who walks with a small limp on his left leg. We lock eyes and I notice that the scared boy in the woods showed the fierce determination that his mother once had.

"Are you ready?" David finally asked.

I breathed in, "I've been ready for years."

"Then what are we waiting for? Let's get it done."

"I couldn't agree more," I said, gesturing for everyone to follow me into the entrance of the Academy.

Vance follows directly behind me along with Kenneth. I unlock the double doors and count down with my fingers from three to allow everyone to initiate the fight. I get down to one and immediately open the doors and my right set of blades. Inside the dimly lit area and corridors are four guards that are taking a patrol around the place. They quickly shift their attention towards us and jump to see us charging inside.

The Runaways run past to overwhelm the stunned guards who prepared for a fight. They are no match for the sheer amount of people with blades that blocked, parried and stabbed them. The guards quickly went down after desperately trying to fight them off. One managed to injure one of our own who is holding his non-bladed shoulder.

David led his own small squad towards communications and medical to raid the supplies and disrupt signals. I take Vance and Kenneth towards the cafeteria, which is left wide open. A couple guards are stationed here, one on either side of the room. The one on the left looks at me funny, puzzled.

"Councilman?" he asked.

"That's me, and I'm relieving you of duty," I responded, walking up to him.

"You're betraying us!" he said.

"No, I'm freeing you," I corrected.

"That's not how I see it," he responded and began to engage.

He gives me no choice, the young guard lunges and I parry with my blades with ease. I elbow him in the face with the same arm coming back from the parry. He stumbled to the ground and quickly tried to get his feet under him. I leave him with no chance and press the two blades into his chest, leaving him stunned and bleeding. He gasped for air and lay flat on the ground.

Kenneth takes down the other guard. In a matter of seconds, the cafeteria is clear. I gesture to Kenneth and Vance to follow once again towards the kitchen in the back. The place is fairly clean, the serving area is emptied out from all the different varieties of food. The stoves are still greasy and charred from either messy or poor cooking. The freezer sits in the corner to the right and the pantry is towards the left. Pots, pans, spatulas and other utensils and dishes are either sitting in the sink or sitting on a shelf on the wall. A vent is hanging up on the wall near the middle of the kitchen.

"Give me a boost up," I told Kenneth.

Kenneth retracts his blades by pulling down his handle, takes a knee and cups his hands to hoist me upward. I plant my foot in his palm and stand on it to reach the vent at head height. Kenneth's hands shake as he keeps me level. I take my blades quickly and pry open the vent like a crowbar. As I rip the vent from the wall, I step down to prevent any injury to Kenneth's hand.

Kenneth shakes his hand, "You wearing rocks under that coat, sir?" he said gritting his teeth.

"It's called muscles, son. I'd learn how to use them," I said in a snarky tone, smiling.

Kenneth had nothing to say as the disbelief filled his face. I face Vance and say, "Alright, just crawl all the way forward and downward. The pipeline is just that way."

"Got it," he said.

I cup my hands this time to provide a step for Vance. He grabs my shoulder for support and plants his foot into my hands. I push and hoist him up into the vent that he manages to fit and crawl into easily. His feet disappear into the opening and I turn to Kenneth.

"Let's get to the pipeline quick," I said, starting to run out of the cafeteria.

Running back around I could see that David and a couple

Runaways are standing near the pipeline entrance with two dead guards beneath them. Their blades stream with blood that drips down onto the floor. The sound of people breaking glass and electrical units is heard at the medical units and communications.

David turned to us, "Did he make it through?"

I nodded, "He should be able to open that door soon."

We wait with blades ready. Seconds go by until the sound of the seal being moved is heard and the door swings open with Vance on the other side. Close behind him are two guards that were sitting in the room.

Me, Kenneth, the Runaways and David pushed into the room, pulling Vance out of the way of danger. There are six guards in here, running towards the entrance. The one closest to me doesn't see me coming and I plunge my foot into his chest, sending him and the others behind him tumbling down the steps.

The guards quickly get up as we move into the room, blades out and ready. There are more of them, which seem to give them more confidence as some give cocky looks. No one moves until one guard lunges at David which he parries just before it reaches his face.

Two of them slash at me in horizontal motions, in which I duck under, possibly cutting some of my stringy hair. I look at them both and hold my blades in front of them. One jabs at me and the other makes a vertical slash. I block the jab and grab the arm of the one making a downward motion with my left hand. I pull him toward my left and make a backhanded slash that he was forced to run into. The blades make a deep gash and the guard plummets to the floor.

The other makes quick slashes, random and ferocious. I parry every one coming too close for comfort. Up, left, right, up again, down, the slashes came all over the place. Finally I push their blades upwards, exposing the torso and sink my blades into their stomach. They stop, take a knee and fall to the ground.

The room falls silent as the guards lay in their own pools of blood. Everyone is gasping for air since the fight took a lot of strength and agility.

Quickly I look at David, "Go cut and loosen the wires. Kenneth, you and the others grab the gasoline and propane from the closet and scatter them around the room."

They all obey and run towards the places I told them to go to. David limps to the wires that he immediately starts cutting with his blades. Kenneth and the other Runaways open the storage unit and pull out green and grey canisters of gasoline and propane.

With everyone working hard to cut wires and pull out tanks of gas, I have to do one other thing. That is to open a gas valve. I look over at the countless workstations where there are various tools. Screws, nails, blowtorches, hammers and more. I am searching for a wrench to unlock the whole pipe.

One sits at the end of one of the workstations and I rapidly take it and head for one of the gas pipes. I stop at a valve that is head height and I immediately start loosening it. I tighten the wrench and push with all my strength. The bolt is tight, almost not budging until I give a little extra force to pry it open. The bolt gives out and I continue to open the valve. I turn on the gas and pull the rest of the bolt out. I yank the pipe open, allowing the gasoline to fill the room with a smell of, of course, gasoline.

I check on David, who is exposing the copper wiring. Until I hear the door slam open. Hunters begin to pour into the room and there are lots of them. At least ten are flooding into the room. All of a sudden I see Vance being held at knifepoint with the head of the Academy holding him.

Vanderbelt holds Vance's shoulder with his non-bladed hand and holds the blades to his neck. Vance's face is filled with fear. His hands shake and his face turns beat red.

The Hunters hold out their blades at us and Vanderbelt yells out, "Step away from the pipes and this will all end in much better circumstances."

# 32

## ROBINS

"What are you doing, Robins? Why are you helping the raid, much less the Runaways? The people you swore to capture," said Vanderbelt.

I am frozen, shaken and building up anger. The Hunters wait patiently for any kind of order, pointing the blades towards us in their fighting stance. Vanderbelt holds his razor sharp blade firm on Vance's neck.

"The system is flawed. We kill innocent people," I said, becoming enraged.

"No, we are eliminating people that have done wrong and they're paying for it," Vanderbelt said in a calm tone.

"They have families, they make up for their wrongdoings. They're not a threat anymore."

"Not a threat?" Vanderbelt laughed, "The medicine man almost killed me by giving the wrong medication."

"People make mistakes! He wasn't trying to do that, Jeffrey is a good man! He's helped people like me!" I retaliated.

"He gave something different for Veisan, too. It seems he only liked to pick favorites."

"Veisan is a drug addict! Jeffrey probably knew that!" I confirmed. The head of security, Veisan, always abused drugs like Valium and narcotics. He was never in the right mindset.

Vanderbelt's face turns into frustration, "Just move away from the gas and leave this room, or I slice this little boy's throat."

My rage is through the roof, it takes all my strength to keep it from being unleashed because I know that if I do anything Vance would die. My face becomes red hot, my knuckles clench so hard that my nails are digging into my palms. My breathing became rapid and my teeth grinded.

"If you do anything to him-" I got no further as Vanderbelt cut me off.

"You'll do what? You're surrounded and have nowhere to go but out of the room," he said.

I want to release all my rage so badly that I thought I couldn't control it anymore. That is until I see Vance move his hand, signaling me to wait. He seemed calm and determined. He points towards his right arm, his bladed arm. The blades that I gave to him before he left the Academy are still in his sleeve.

I stalled, "I assume you were the one placing the false bounties? Why blame it on me?"

Vanderbelt laughed, "Not false, they were official. The bounties were carried out and we made money. But, you're also the councilman that's supposed to carry these out, so it was easy to say that the orders came from you. But why would that matter? You've placed bounties on others you're working with now. Like young David over there," he said, pointing towards David who is also frozen still.

"That was a mistake," I said.

"Oh, a mistake, huh? You put this young man through hell and now he trusts you? Tell me boy, why are you working with him after all the things he has done to you. He wanted you dead, thrown away like trash. Why would you work with him," he asked David.

David hesitates and looks over at me and back at Vanderbelt with much anger, "Because he's not the one that killed my mother."

Vanderbelt had no other words to say.

"Robins is a good man, I know I didn't realize that until recently. But he wants us free. And he has a condition, you see. He can't control it and he really wants to unleash it now. Once you realize that the boy you're holding is actually supposed to be the one that was executed, he'll tear you to shreds," David said confidently.

Vanderbelt looks down, confused at what David was talking about. Vance reveals his blades and stabs them straight through Vanderbelt's forearm, tearing flesh and severing tendons. Vanderbilt cries out in pain as the blood gushes out from his bladed arm.

Vance moves away and my rage immediately falls out of control. I unlock my second set of blades and I scream out in sheer anger and fury. The first two Hunters are taken down in one quick swing, they are no match for the sheer amount of strength and force that I put upon them. They laid flat on their backs, revealing two large gashes in their chests.

I move on to the next ones. Four come swinging at me, one makes a horizontal swing, another does a quick jab, the next makes another horizontal swing to my left and the last forces a jab on my right. I move forward and parry the jab in front of me with my left and block the swing in front with my right. The two on my sides miss as I shift forward.

I stabbed the Hunter that I blocked with my left and quickly turned to the rest. The one I parried swung back to my face and I blocked with both my blades. The one on my left swings to the back of my head and I duck, making them slice the one I was currently blocking directly in the face. They quickly go down and behind them is the other Hunter that missed the first shot and came in with a full thrust.

I go right under their blades and push up with my blades into their chest, lifting them up off the ground. I slam them onto the ground and turn around to the very last one. They come swinging in multiple areas and I quickly block one with my left and stab them in the torso with my right. I bash them down to the ground and pull out my blades that are dripping with blood.

I could see David and Kenneth holding their own. Kenneth blocks and parries most that come towards David. David struggles to keep standing from all the massive blows. The other runaways are desperately trying to stay alive while help comes into the room, telling them that they have to leave. Vanderbelt stood up, holding his arm that was still gushing out blood.

I know that the wires are set and the gas is still filling the room. There is only one more action left, and that is turning on the emergency power which is sitting on the wall close to the main entrance. I need to get my allies out of the building first.

"Vance! Kenneth! David! Get out!" I screamed.

As Kenneth finally defeats the last Hunter, he looks over and yells, "What about you?"

"Just go!" I screamed back, looking back at Vanderbelt.

They begin to take off out of the room and Vance hesitates to leave once they get to the exit. He looks back, fear filling his face and lips quivering. I gesture for him to leave and Kenneth pulls him away from the door.

I engage Vanderbelt, who seems too weak to stand now. Once I get close enough, he swings with his crippled hand. I easily block it with my left and give a ferocious stab in his stomach. His face squints in agony.

I push him with my blades towards the emergency power

and slam him against the wall. I retract my left blades, take the handle for the power, and wait for the rest of the Runaways to get out. They sprint and dash through the exit and I continue to give them time to leave.

"You'll never escape," Vanderbelt grunted.

I look down at him, adrenaline pumping and heart beating rapidly. My hand shook and I could barely breathe.

"Watch me," I respond, and I take the lever and pull it down. The sparks fly from the copper wiring and flames blow through the air, causing the gas canisters to explode and erupt in fire. It is done, the very last mission that I set is complete.

# DAVID

The ground rumbles and shakes ferociously, the force of the whole pipeline pushes me and everyone else that is getting out of the building down to the ground. Fire bursts through the windows, glass flies in all directions, the bricks that make up the walls of the Academy crack and fall apart. The structure of the building collapses and people scatter around the area.

I move with Vance, pulling him off the ground and away from all the destruction. The building continues to explode and cast debris everywhere. Shards of glass pass by my face and bricks land just behind me.

Vance, the man called Kenneth and I run as fast as we can towards the other side of the block. Others follow suit and take cover behind other buildings and objects. I continue to run until I notice Vance has stopped running.

Vance is standing in the middle of the road, staring at the burning building. His legs wobble and he falls on his knees. Behind me I could hear the cheers and cries of the Runaways that made it back alive, joyful that they have finally vanquished the Academy.

I run over to Vance, making sure he is alright. "Vance, are you alright?" I yelled.

Vance stands there with a tear running down his face, "He . . . he promised . . . he said he'd come back."

His lips quiver, tears fall and his body shakes. The one person that seemed to care for him as a father was gone. I could tell they were close in the short amount of time I saw them together. Robins would've done anything to protect him, and when I saw that Vance's life was being threatened I knew Robins would do whatever it took to save him.

"He saved us, Vance. I'm sorry, but there's nothing that we can do," I said.

Vance says nothing, just stares at the blaze growing on the burning structure. I could hear sirens off into the distance. That, I thought, was our cue to leave.

"Kenneth, we need to leave before anyone else shows up," I said.

Kenneth nods in understanding and grabs Vance, putting him over his shoulder. He yells for everyone to take the Sweepers and head back. The Runaways do not hesitate and immediately run for their vehicles, which is fairly close to the fire. They aren't damaged significantly. One has a brick that hit the window but didn't shatter it and instead cracked it. I follow Kenneth into his Sweeper along with Vance.

Kenneth starts the car and begins to follow the rest of the group that heads back towards the mountains. Vance still looks back at the inferno, still absolutely paralyzed by what had happened. The car moves onto the road, and towards the trees that are past the train station. The fire and smoke begins to dissipate along with the rest of the town once we hit the treeline.

///

The trek upwards is longer than I remember. We hide the Sweepers in a divot at the bottom of the mountain and cover it with green tarps that camouflaged with the grass and undergrowth. Scaling the mountain is hard with all the injured that came back, stumbling and falling onto the ground.

However, we manage to reach the camp that sits in the cave above. Kenneth helps carry some people uphill. I assist him until we get to the top. Sandra immediately starts tending to the wounded along with two other people to help, a man and woman.

Linda stands near the fire that I woke up by. She is standing, wrapped up in a large blanket. She looks much more healthy, but she still wears a bandage on her head. She looks over at us and sees me. She smiles and comes running towards me.

I sprint for her and wrap my arms around her and give her a squeeze. After a couple seconds of a huge hug, she grabs my face and presses her lips against mine. I kiss her back, relieved that we made it back and that she is alright.

"It's over, we don't need to hide anymore. The Academy is gone," I said excitedly.

She smirked, "So we got all the way up here for nothing?" she said in a joking manner.

I laughed, "Well, we're here and that's all that matters."

"Agreed," Linda said.

We lock eyes once again, looking directly into her gorgeous eyes. I couldn't imagine nor describe better beauty. I couldn't look away.

"I'll start helping them," she finally said.

"Oh . . . uh . . . yeah, I'll help as well," I said awkwardly, probably cracking my voice a little bit.

She smiles and turns to help pack up tents. Turning around I could see Vance once again staring out into the distance at the tiny cloud of smoke coming from the Academy. I walk over, stand right beside him and hold onto his shoulder for comfort.

"He was the closest thing I had to a father," he said.

I feel sympathy for Vance but also shameful for thinking of Robins in a completely different way.

"Of course he had his problems but he still took care of me," he continued.

"He was a good man," I began. Vance looks up at me,

listening to what I have to say. "I didn't get to understand him like you did. When this whole thing started I was terrified of him and I hated him for what he was doing. I thought he truly wanted to hurt us."

I pause, choking up on my words. "Now I know what he was trying to do. It was hard, but you and him opened my eyes to your side of the story. I know his perspective now. Now we don't have to worry about the Academy ever again, and he did that for us. Not just for his beliefs."

Vance peers down at the ground, watching his tears drop to the rocks. "I think we should honor him by making the best of it. He did that so that we could live, let's listen to him."

Vance wipes away his tears, looks up at me, and nods in agreement.

It is true, I never got to see Robins' perspective. All I did was focus on what I thought and what mattered to me. I now want to make sure that I will focus on others and what story they have to tell. Not just mine.

"There is no great good or great evil, there is only perspective."

# ABOUT THE AUTHOR

**EZEKIEL ELIZALDE** was born in 2001 in Austin, Texas. Growing up in Kyle and Buda, Texas, he has been surrounded by movies and stories such as Journey to the Center of the Earth and has even been inspired to write graphic novels in middle and high school with his best friends. He likes to play video games and spend time with his family and friends. *Rage, Refuge, and Rebellion* is Ezekiel's first book.